WESTERN **WP** PROMISES

WESTERN **WP** PROMISES

Daddy's Double Duty

STELLA BAGWELL

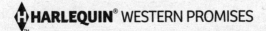

HARLEQUIN® WESTERN PROMISES

Recycling programs
for this product may
not exist in your area.

ISBN-13: 978-0-373-00375-4

Daddy's Double Duty

Printed in U.S.A.

www.Harlequin.com

After writing more than eighty books for Harlequin, **Stella Bagwell** still finds it exciting to create new stories and bring her characters to life. She loves all things Western and has been married to her own real cowboy for forty-four years. Living on the south Texas coast, she also enjoys being outdoors and helping her husband care for the horses, cats and dog that call their small ranch home. The couple has one son, who teaches high school mathematics and is also an athletic director. Stella loves hearing from readers. They can contact her at stellabagwell@gmail.com.

Books by Stella Bagwell

Harlequin Special Edition

Men of the West
Daddy Wore Spurs
The Lawman's Noelle
Wearing the Rancher's Ring
One Tall, Dusty Cowboy
A Daddy for Dillon
The Baby Truth
The Doctor's Calling
His Texas Baby
Christmas with the Mustang Man
His Medicine Woman
Daddy's Double Duty
His Texas Wildflower
The Deputy's Lost and Found
Branded with His Baby
Lone Star Daddy

Montana Mavericks: Striking It Rich
Paging Dr. Right

The Fortunes of Texas
The Heiress and the Sheriff

Visit the Author Profile page at Harlequin.com for more titles.

To my late father,
Louis Copeland Cook,
who always said don't do anything
unless you intend to do it right.
I hope he thinks I have.

Chapter One

His secretary was crying!

Conall Donovan stared at the woman behind the cherrywood desk. Vanessa Valdez had been in his employ for more than two months and during that time she'd been nothing but cool and professional. He could hardly imagine what had brought about these waterworks. In the past hour, he hadn't even yelled once! And even if he had, it wouldn't have been directed at her. She was the epitome of a perfect, professional secretary.

Cautiously, he approached the desk. "Vanessa? Is something wrong?"

With one slender hand dabbing a tissue to

her cheek, the petite brunette glanced at him. At thirty-five, she looked more like twenty-five, Conall thought. And though he wouldn't describe her as gorgeous, she was an attractive woman with honey-brown hair brushing the tops of her shoulders and curling in pretty wisps around her head. Usually, her large brown eyes were soft and luminous but presently her eyes were full of tears.

"I'm sorry," she said in a strained voice. "It's... I... Something has happened."

"Your father? Has he taken ill?" he demanded.

Vanessa paused and he could see her throat working as she tried to swallow. The sight of her discomposure struck him unexpectedly hard. In spite of her being an old family acquaintance, they hardly shared a close bond. For the most part, the woman kept to herself. The only reason he knew she'd lost her mother two years ago, and that her aging father now resided in a nursing home, was because he happened to attend the same small church where her parents had been regular members. Still, these past months, Vanessa had become a quiet and dependable fixture in his life and he'd come to respect her dedication to this job and the subtle finesse she used with clients in order to make his life easier.

"No," she answered. "It's not my father."

When she failed to elaborate, Conall fought back an impatient sigh. He hardly had time to play mind reader.

"Do you need to take the rest of the afternoon off?" he asked bluntly. There was still a hell of a lot of work that he needed finished by the end of the day, but if necessary he'd somehow manage without her. Even if it meant calling on his mother, Fiona, to fill in for the remainder of the afternoon.

Shaking her head, his secretary sniffed and tried to straighten her shoulders. Even so, Conall could see tears sparkling upon her smooth cheeks and he was shocked at the sudden urge he felt to round the desk and wipe them away.

Hell, Conall, you've never been good at consoling women. Just ask your ex-wife. Besides, women and tears don't affect your iron heart. Not anymore.

While he shoved that unbidden thought away, she finally answered in a ragged voice, "I—I'll be all right, Conall. Just give me a few moments to…get over the shock."

Shock? As usual, the phone had been ringing all afternoon. The Diamond D Ranch was a huge conglomerate, with business connections all over the world. With it being the middle of summer, they were in the busy height of Thoroughbred racing season. His office was only one of several set in a modern brick building situated north of the ranch yard and west of the main ranch house. His younger brother Liam, the ranch's horse trainer, also had his own office along with a secretary, and then there was the general accounting for the ranch, which took up several rooms. As for Conall's job, he rarely saw a quiet moment during working hours and the overflow of correspondence kept his secretary extremely busy. Especially now that he'd also assumed the job of keeping the Golden Spur Mine operations running smoothly.

"Look, Vanessa, I realize I'm asking you to handle an undue amount of work for one human being. But it won't always be like this. I have plans to hire an assistant for you, just as soon as I have a chance to go over a few résumés."

Her brown eyes widened even more. "Oh, no, Conall, it's not the work!" She gestured toward the piles of correspondence lying about on her desk. "I can easily handle this. I just received a call from Las Vegas," she attempted to explain. "It was…horrible news. A dear friend has passed away. And I…well, I just can't believe she's gone. She was—"

Suddenly sobs overtook the remainder of her words and Conall could no longer stop himself from skirting the desk and taking a steadying hold on her trembling shoulders.

"I'm very sorry, Vanessa."

Averting her face from him, she whispered, "I'm okay. Really, I am."

Whether she was trying to reassure him or herself, or the both of them, Conall didn't know. In any case, she was clearly an emotional wreck and he had to do something to help her, even if it was wrong.

"No, you're hardly okay," he said gruffly. "You're shaking. Let me help you over to the couch."

With firm hands, he drew her up from the rolling desk chair and with an arm at her waist, guided her to a long leather couch positioned along the far wall.

"Just sit and try to relax," he ordered as he eased her small frame down. "I'll be back in a minute."

Once she was safely settled, Conall hurriedly crossed the room and stepped into his private office, where he kept an assortment of drinks to offer visiting businessmen. After pouring a mug half-full of coffee, he splashed in a hefty amount of brandy and carried it out to her.

"Here," he told her. "Drink this. All of it."

With trembling hands wrapped around the heavy cup, she tilted the contents to her lips. After a few careful sips that made her gasp and cough, she lowered it and cast him an accusing glance.

"That has alcohol in it!"

"Not nearly enough," he said dryly.

"It's more than enough for me." Straightening her shoulders, she offered the cup back to him. "Thank you. I can talk now."

Relieved to see a faint bit of color returning to her face, Conall took the cup and after placing it on the floor, he eased down beside her. "All right," he said gently. "Tell me what happened to your friend."

Closing her eyes, she pressed slender fingers against her forehead. Conall couldn't help but notice the long sweep of her lashes as they settled against her damp cheeks. Her complexion reminded him of a pink pearl bathed in golden sunlight and not for the first time he thought how her skin was the most fetching thing about her. Smooth and kissable.

Now why the hell was he thinking that sort of thing, especially at a time like this? Kissing a woman's soft skin was all in his past. And that was where it was going to stay.

With her eyes still closed, she began to speak. "I became friends with Hope Benson not long after I arrived in Las Vegas. We both worked as cocktail waitresses in the Lucky Treasure casino."

Conall was stunned. He'd not known that Vanessa had ever worked as a cocktail waitress. Not that it mattered. Everyone had to start somewhere. And she'd obviously climbed the ladder. A few months ago, when she'd left Nevada, she'd been a private secretary to a casino executive.

"I didn't realize you ever worked as a waitress," he mused, speaking his thoughts out loud.

The guttural sound in her throat was self-deprecating. "What did you expect, Conall? I left Hondo Valley with nothing. It took lots of long, hard hours to put myself through college."

Of course he'd known that Vanessa was from a poor family. She was the same age as his sister Maura, and the two women had been good friends ever since elementary school. During those years, Vanessa had often visited the ranch. Being two years older, Conall hadn't paid much attention to her. With the house full of six Donovan kids, there were always plenty of friends hanging around and Vanessa had simply been one more. The main thing he recalled about her was that she'd been very quiet, almost to the point of being a wallflower.

After Conall had gone away to college, he'd heard in passing that Vanessa had moved to Nevada. That had been fifteen years ago and since then he'd not heard anything else about his sister's old friend. In fact, she'd completely slipped his mind until two months ago, when she'd called him about the secretarial job.

She'd moved back to Hondo Valley to stay, she'd told him, and she was looking for a job. He was secretly ashamed to admit that he'd not expected Vanessa to be qualified. As a teenager, she'd seemed like the shy, homemaker sort, who'd want to devote her life to raising a house full of kids and keeping a husband happy. He couldn't imagine her as a career woman. But out of courtesy to his sister, he'd invited her to come out to the ranch for an interview. When she'd walked into his office,

Conall had been stunned to see a very professional young woman presenting him with an equally impressive résumé. He'd hired her on the spot and since that time had not once regretted his decision.

The soft sigh escaping her lips caught his attention and he watched her eyes open, then level on his face. For the moment her tears had disappeared, but in their place he saw something that amounted to panic. A strange emotion to be experiencing over a friend's demise, he couldn't help thinking.

"Sorry," she said. "I didn't mean to sound defensive. God knows how He's blessed me. And now... I just don't know what to think, Conall. You see, Hope was pregnant. Something happened after she went into labor—I'm not exactly sure what. The lawyer didn't go into details. Except that she had to have an emergency C-section. Shortly afterward, she died from some sort of complications. I assume it had something to do with her heart condition—a genetic childhood thing. But she always appeared healthy and I thought the doctors were keeping everything under control. In fact, each time I'd talked with her, she'd assured me that she and the babies were doing fine."

Conall's attention latched on to one word. "Babies? Are you talking plural?"

Vanessa nodded. "Twins. A boy and a girl. They were born three days ago and Hope's lawyer has just now had a chance to go over the legalities of her will and wishes."

"And what does this have to do with you?" Conall asked.

Across the room the telephone on Vanessa's desk began to ring. She started to rise to answer it, but Conall caught her shoulder with a firm hand. "Forget the phone," he ordered. "Whoever it is will call back or leave a message. I want to hear the rest of this."

Groaning, Vanessa dropped her head and shook it back and forth as though she was in a dream. "It's unbelievable, Conall! Hope wanted me to have custody of her babies. I—I'm to be their mother."

"Mother?" The word burst from Conall's mouth before he could stop it. "Are you...serious?"

Her head shot up and for a brief moment she scowled at him. "Very serious. Why? Do you think I'm incapable of being a mother?"

A grimace tightened his lips. Leave it to a woman to misread his words, he thought. "I don't doubt your abilities, Vanessa. I'm sure you have...great motherly instincts. I was questioning the validity of your friend's wishes. Isn't the father around?"

Her shoulders slumped as she thrust a shaky hand through her hair. "The father was only in Hope's life for a brief period before they went their separate ways. When she learned that she was pregnant, she contacted him with the news, but he wanted nothing to do with her or the babies. Seems as though he was already paying a hefty amount of child support to his ex-wife and he wasn't keen on adding more to his responsibilities. By then Hope had already come to the conclusion that he wasn't the sort of man she'd ever want back in her life. And she certainly didn't want him to have any claims to the babies. When she confronted him with legal documents, he was only too glad to sign away his parental rights."

"What a bastard," Conall muttered.

Vanessa sighed. "I knew she was making a mistake when she first got involved with the creep. But she really fell hard for him. Poor thing, she believed he loved her and she desperately wanted a big family. You see, she was adopted and didn't have many relatives."

"What about her parents?"

"If you mean her real parents, she never

looked for them. She considered the Bensons to be her true parents. But when Hope was still very young, they were killed in the Loma Prieta earthquake in California," she said ruefully. "Luckily, Hope escaped being physically injured, but I don't think she ever got over the emotional loss of her parents."

"Damn. Sounds like your friend didn't have an easy life."

"No. Life is never easy for some," she sadly agreed. "Hope was forty-two. She figured this would be her last and only chance to have children. That's why she risked carrying the babies. Even though doctors had warned her about being pregnant with her type of heart condition, she wanted them desperately."

"Had you discussed any of this with your friend?" Conall asked. "I mean, about you becoming their mother if something happened to her?"

Vanessa nodded glumly. "At the very beginning of her pregnancy Hope asked me to be their godmother. I agreed. How could I not? The two of us had been good friends for a long time. We…went through some tough times together. And I wanted to reassure her that no matter what, I'd see that the babies would be well cared for. But I also kept telling her that she was going to be okay—that everything with her and the babies would be fine. I wanted her to concentrate on the future she was going to have with her children." Tears once again filled her eyes. "Oh, Conall, I didn't think… I refused to believe that Hope might die."

Conall hated himself for not knowing the right words to ease the grief that was clearly ripping her apart. But he'd learned with Nancy that he wasn't good at dealing with women's problems.

"None of us ever wants to consider losing someone we're close to, Vanessa. But we can't go around thinking the worst. Where would that get us?"

Where indeed, Vanessa wondered dazedly. Swallowing at the painful lump in her throat, she rose to her feet and wandered aimlessly across the room.

For years now, she'd desperately wanted children. But as she'd struggled to obtain a degree in business management, she'd set aside having a family. Then when she'd finally achieved that goal, she'd slowly begun to work her way off the casino floor and into the business offices. First as a simple file clerk, then on to secretarial assistant, then a jump to office manager, and finally a great leap to personal secretary to the CEO of Lucky Treasures. During that climb, she'd met her now ex-husband, and she'd believed her dreams of having a family of her own were finally going to become a reality. But Jeff had turned out to be nothing but a hanger-on, a man only too happy to let his wife support him while he went his free and fancy way.

Vanessa supposed it was a good thing that children had never come from their short marriage. But since the divorce, she'd grieved long and hard for what hadn't been and prayed that someday her fate would change. Still, she'd never expected to become a mother in this shocking fashion and the news was almost too much for her to absorb.

"I suppose you're right, Conall. We can't dwell on what might go wrong. But I—" She stopped in front of the huge picture window that framed a view of the mountain ridge that ran along the north edge of the massive horse ranch. "Right now I'm...stunned. In the next few days, the lawyer expects me to be in Vegas to pick up the babies! There's so much I'm going to have to do! I live in my parents' house. Do you remember it?"

Vaguely, Conall thought. It had been a long time since he'd driven through that mountainous area northeast of the Diamond D, but he did recall the tiny stucco home where the Valdez family had resided for so many years. The place had always needed work. And to give him credit, Mr. Valdez had done the best he could on a carpenter's salary. But his four sons had been the worthless sort, never lifting a hand to help their parents or themselves. As far as Conall knew, Vanessa's brothers were all gone from the area now and all he could think was good riddance. She didn't need any of them trying to mooch her hard-earned money.

"Yes, I remember," Conall told her. "Are you living there by yourself? I mean, do you have enough extra room to accommodate the babies?"

"It's just me living there," she replied, "so there's enough room. But the place isn't equipped to handle two infants! You see, I came back to Hondo Valley, so that I'd be around to see after my father's needs. I know he has great medical care in the nursing home, but he needs my emotional support—especially now that Mama is gone. And since I'm divorced now I never dreamed about raising a family there! Dear heaven, there are so many things I'll have to change—buy—to make a nursery for the babies!"

She jerked with surprise when she felt his hands fold over the back of her shoulders. She'd not heard him walk up behind her, but even if she'd been warned of his approach, his touch would have been just as jolting to her senses. Conall Donovan was like no man she'd ever known. For a time, when she'd been a sophomore in high school and he a senior, she'd had an enormous crush on him. He'd been one of those rare guys who'd possessed brains and brawn. He'd also been a perfect gentleman, who'd been nothing but nice and polite to his sister's poor friend. Now after all these years, he was her employer, and she'd done her best to forget about the crush. Until a few minutes ago, when he'd touched her for the very first time.

"Tell me, Vanessa, do you want these babies in your life?"

The question caused her to whirl around to face him and just as quickly she wished she'd kept her back to him. The man's presence was always overwhelming, but up close like this, it was downright rattling her already ragged senses.

Nearly black hair lay in undisciplined waves about his head, while one errant hank teased a cool gray eye that peered at her beneath a heavy black brow. His features were large, rough and edged with a haggardness that could only come from working long, hard hours without enough rest. His clothes, which ranged from faded jeans to designer suits, always fit his tall, well-honed body as though they'd been tailored for him. And probably had been, she thought wryly. He was certainly rich enough to afford such an extravagance.

As far as Vanessa was concerned, she always thought of Conall Donovan as dark, dangerous and delicious. And something totally beyond her reach. And standing only inches away from him like this only reinforced those descriptions of the man.

Nervously licking her lips, she attempted to answer his question. "Of course I want the babies! There's nothing I want more." She didn't tell him that during her short marriage she'd wanted children, but her husband had insisted he loved her too much to want to share her with a child. Now Vanessa very nearly gagged when she thought of how phony those words had been. Jeff hadn't loved her. He'd only loved himself. But Conall didn't want to hear about the personal mistakes she'd made. Besides, they were far too humiliating to share with a man like him.

"I've always wanted children. And I want Hope's twins to be loved. I'm positive that I can give them that love and raise them as if I gave birth to them myself. But I'm not sure how I can handle all the changes I need to make right now. I have very little time and—"

"Whoa! Slow down, Vanessa. Let's take one thing at a time," he said. "What do you need to do first?"

Behind her, the phone began to ring again, but the subtle change in his expression was telling her to, once again, forget the telephone.

Turning her palms upward, she tried to breathe normally and assure herself that this man's sexual aura wasn't going to suffocate her. "I suppose the first thing is to go to Vegas and collect the babies. They've already been released from the hospital and placed in temporary care at a Catholic orphanage."

With a dour frown, he turned away from her and began to pace back and forth in front of her desk. Momentarily relieved by the space between them, Vanessa drew in a much-needed breath.

"I'm sure they're being well cared for," he said suddenly. "But I'm certain you'll feel better once we fetch the children back here as soon as possible."

We? Where had that come from? This was her problem. Not his. But that wasn't entirely true, she reminded herself. Conall was depending on her to keep his office running smoothly. Bringing two infants all the way from Vegas and getting them settled was going to chop into her work time. Naturally, this whole thing was going to affect him, too, she thought sickly. And what was that going to do to her job? A job that she'd quickly come to love, and now, more than ever, desperately needed.

"I'm sorry, Conall. I suppose I'll have to ask for time off while I make arrangements to fly out and collect the twins. If you feel you need to let me go permanently," she added ruefully, "then I'll understand."

Stopping in his tracks, he scowled at her. "Let you go? What the hell, Vanessa? Do you think Donovans fire our employees whenever they need help?"

Seeing she'd offended him, she drew in a deep breath and blew it out. "I didn't mean it like that. You obviously have tons of work to deal with. You can't do it alone and you put your trust in me to be here every day. I can't expect you to suffer just because I have a problem."

He waved a dismissive hand through the air.

"This isn't like you're asking for time off to go on a shopping binge or some other frivolous excursion," he barked, then resumed pacing. "I'll deal with the problems here in the office. Mother will step in your place for the time being. As for me, I suppose I could ask Dad to deal with my most pressing obligations. He doesn't know anything about the mining business. But he can always call me with questions," he went on, more to himself than to her. "I'll discuss this with my parents tonight. In the meantime, you get on the phone and buy plane tickets for tomorrow. You can be ready by then, can't you?"

Vanessa was accustomed to his rapid-fire orders. Some days he rattled them off as though she were a tape recorder. But this afternoon, she'd been knocked off-kilter and the sudden personal attention Conall was giving her wasn't helping her brain snap into action. She stared at him with confusion.

"Tickets? Pardon me, Conall, but I only need one round-trip ticket."

Walking back to her, he held up two fingers. "You need to purchase two tickets. I'm going with you."

She gasped and he smiled.

"What's wrong?" he asked. "Afraid you'll

fall asleep on the plane and I'll see you with your mouth open?"

Was he saying something about her mouth? she wondered fuzzily. And had something gone wrong with the room's thermostat? Sweat was popping out on her forehead and upper lip. Her legs felt oddly weak and there was a loud rushing noise in her ears.

"Conall— I—"

The remainder of her words were never uttered as she slumped forward and straight into his arms.

Chapter Two

"Poor little thing. The shock must have gotten to her."

From somewhere above her, Vanessa could hear Fiona Donovan's concerned voice, but try as she might, she couldn't open her eyes or form one word.

"Her pulse is getting stronger. She's coming around."

This statement came from Bridget Donovan, the doctor of the family. Vanessa could feel the pressure of the young woman's fingers wrapped around her wrist.

"Well, if the truth be known, Conall probably forced her to work through lunch," Fiona continued in an accusing tone. "She probably hasn't had a bite to eat all day."

"Mom, I don't force Vanessa to do anything," Conall said brusquely. "She probably stopped long enough to eat a sandwich or some of that gooey stuff from a carton that she seems to favor."

"You don't know whether she ate or not?" Fiona shot back at her son.

"Hell, no! I've been in my office since before daylight and didn't come out until a few minutes ago when I found her crying. I don't know about her lunch! But you can see she's not starving. She has plenty of meat on her bones."

His last remark was enough to spike Vanessa's blood pressure and with a weak groan, she slowly opened her eyes to see she was lying on the couch in her office. Bridget was kneeling over her, while Conall and his mother stood just behind the young doctor.

"Hello, pretty lady," Bridget said with a bright smile. "Glad to see you're back with the living."

Vanessa's fuzzy eyesight darted over the redheaded doctor and then slowly progressed up to Conall's dour face. Next to him, Fiona was smiling with happy relief.

"What…happened?" Vanessa asked weakly. "I was talking to Conall and the next thing I knew there was a strange rushing noise in my ears."

"You fainted," Bridget explained. "Thankfully Conall caught you before you hit your head on the desk or the floor. When he called over to the house for help, I happened to be home on a break from the clinic. How are you feeling now?"

"Weak and groggy," Vanessa admitted. "But better."

"Good. Your color is returning," she said. "Conall tells me you received a bit of a shock about your friend."

"Yes. I was feeling a bit shaky, but I never dreamed I'd do anything like…faint! This is so embarrassing." She glanced back at Conall to see his expression was still grim and she figured he had to be terribly annoyed for all this interference in his work schedule. Over the past couple of months, she'd learned his work was his life and he didn't appreciate anything or anyone intervening. "I'm sorry, Conall. I've disrupted the whole office and your family."

"Nonsense!" Fiona blurted out before her son had a chance to utter a word. "You had every right to have a little fainting spell. Most women have nine months to prepare to be a mother. From what Conall tells us, you didn't have nine minutes."

"I'm just glad I happened to be home," Bridget quickly added. "Conall feared you were having a heart attack." She clamped a strong hand on Vanessa's shoulder. "Sit up for me and let's see how you do now."

With the young woman's help, Vanessa rose to a sitting position. "I'm fine. Really," she told the doctor. "I feel much stronger now and my head isn't whirling."

"Well, from what I can see, you had a simple, garden-variety faint. It happens to the best of us sometimes," Bridget assured her. "But if you have any more trouble—weakness, dizziness or anything like that—please get to your doctor for a checkup. Okay?"

"Yes. I promise. Thank you, Bridget."

"No problem," she said, then with a broad smile, she rose to a standing position and pointed a direct look at her brother. "I've got to get back to the clinic, so I'm leaving the patient in your hands, Conall. You might go lightly on her the remainder of the day."

"Vanna is going to get the rest of the afternoon off," Fiona spoke up, using the shortened name that Maura had given Vanessa many years ago when the two had been teenagers. "In fact, Conall is going to drive her home."

Vanessa opened her mouth to argue, but quickly decided not to make the effort. Fiona could be just as formidable as her son and with Bridget agreeing that Vanessa could clearly use some rest, she had no choice but to go along with the family's wishes.

Once Bridget had departed the small office, Conall said to Vanessa, "I'll get your things and we'll be on our way."

While Conall collected her sweater and handbag from a tiny closet located in the short hallway separating her office from his, Fiona was already taking a seat at Vanessa's desk.

"While you two are gone," she said to Conall, "I'll take care of the plane tickets and see to organizing anything else you might need for the trip to Vegas. If there are still empty seats, do you want the first flight out?"

"That would be great, Mom. See what you can do."

With her things thrown over his arm, he walked over to the couch and slipped a hand beneath Vanessa's elbow.

"Think you can stand okay now?" he asked gently.

Since she'd gone to work for this tall, dark

powerhouse of a man, he'd been polite enough to her, but mostly he was all business. It felt more than strange to have him addressing her about personal things and even more unsettling to have him touching her.

"Yes," she assured him, then feeling her cheeks warm with an embarrassed flush, added, "I don't think you need worry about having to catch me again."

Not bothering to make a reply, he began to guide her toward the door. Across the room, Fiona flung a parting question at her son.

"Conall, the hotel rooms. How many nights do you need reserved? Or do you have any idea about that?"

"No idea," he said. "Better leave that open."

"Right," she replied, then tossed a reassuring smile at Vanessa. "Don't worry, Vanna. Everything is going to be just fine. Why, in no time you'll have those little babies of yours home and in your arms."

Vanessa thanked the woman for her kind thoughts and then Conall ushered her out to a shiny black pickup truck with the Diamond D brand emblazoned on the doors.

After he'd helped her into the cab and they were barreling past a fenced paddock filled with a row of busy mechanical horse walkers, he said, "You gave me a fright back there when you fainted. Are you sure you're okay?"

He was staring straight ahead and Vanessa could read little from his granite-etched profile. For the most part, she'd always thought of him as an unfeeling man, but maybe that was because he didn't allow his feelings to show on his face. He was certainly going out of his way to help her. Which created an even bigger question in her mind. Why? Even if she was his one and only secretary, her personal problems were none of his responsibility.

"I'm okay, Conall. Really. I just feel…silly for causing you and your family so much trouble." Her gaze turned toward the passenger window as they curved away from the Donovan ranch house. The structure's stalwart appearance hadn't changed since she'd left the Hondo Valley more than fifteen years ago. And she liked to think the big Irish family that lived inside hadn't changed, either—that if she stepped inside, she'd still feel like Cinderella visiting the castle.

"Forget it," he practically snapped.

She looked at him. "But you—"

He interrupted before she could say more. "Let it rest, Vanessa."

Sighing, she smoothed the hem of her skirt

over her knees and stared ahead. One minute everything had been going along fine. As fine as it could be for a divorced woman with her family split in all directions and an aging father too debilitated from a stroke to leave the nursing home. Yet those problems seemed small in comparison to what she was facing now.

Still, Vanessa realized she couldn't give in to the overwhelming shock. She had to straighten her shoulders and take up the reins of her life again. But taking them out of Conall's hands was not going to be an easy task. He was a man who was all about using his power to bend operations to his liking. And she was all about independence. She didn't want to be beholden to anyone and that included her boss. Yet this was one time that agreeing to a little help might be the sensible thing for her to do. Especially for the babies' sake.

"You don't like accepting help from anyone, do you?" he asked as he steered the truck off Diamond D ranch land and onto the main highway.

The man must be a mind reader, she thought. "I like taking care of myself," she answered truthfully, then realizing how ungrateful that probably sounded to him, she glanced over and added, "But this is one time I can't take care of things entirely on my own. And I am grateful to you, Conall. Please know that."

He didn't say anything for a while and she was wondering if she'd offended him, when he said, "You can tell me if I'm getting too personal, Vanessa, but what about your brothers? If I remember right, you had four of them. Are any of them close enough to help you with the babies?"

Vanessa choked back a mocking laugh. Her brothers couldn't care for themselves, much less two needy babies. "My brothers all moved far away from here. They conveniently forgot their parents and only sister. And that's fine with me, 'cause I wouldn't ask them for the time of day," she said flatly.

"That's too bad."

She heaved out a heavy breath. "It's probably for the best, Conall. None of them have ever made much effort to become responsible men. The only one who comes close to it is Michael—the one your age. And he's hardly in the running for sainthood," she added.

He didn't make any sort of reply to that and Vanessa figured he was thinking badly of her. The Donovan family had always been a strong unit. They lived together, worked and played together, and stuck close even when life's problems crashed in unexpectedly. He probably couldn't understand why she and her brothers lacked the love and devotion it took to keep the Valdez family bonded. But then, she'd never understood it herself.

"Sorry," she said quietly. "I didn't mean to sound so…judgmental. But believe me when I say there are no relatives around to help. Not with the babies, my father, the home place, anything."

In other words, she had her hands full, Conall thought grimly. As he'd suspected, the Valdez brothers had left Lincoln County. He'd not seen any of them in years and even when they had still been around, Conall hadn't associated with any of them. He'd never been into strutting around in black leather and begging for scrapes with the law. Some time back, he'd heard the eldest son had served time for distributing drugs over in El Paso, but as far as he knew, no gossip had ever surfaced about the remaining three.

Conall cast a brief glance at her. What had her life been like these past years she'd been away from the valley? She'd certainly climbed the workforce ladder. But in spite of her having more financial security, she was more or less alone in life. Like him.

Which only proved that riches didn't always come in the form of money, he thought.

Ten minutes later, on a five-acre tract of land near the tiny settlement of Tinnie, Conall pulled the truck to a stop in front of a rickety picket fence. Beyond the whitewashed barrier was a small stucco house of faded turquoise. One mesquite tree shaded the front entrance, while a short rock walkway crossed a bare dirt yard. A brown-and-white nanny goat stood on the porch as she reared on her hind legs and nipped at a hanging pot of red geraniums.

Even though he'd not been by the homestead recently, the Valdez home looked pretty much as it always had. Seeing the family's modest existence normally wouldn't have affected Conall one way or the other. Rich and poor was a fact of life. Not just in the New Mexico mountains, but everywhere. Yet now that he was beginning to know Vanessa, he was struck by the stark simplicity of the place. She'd left a very high-paying job to return to this, he thought incredibly. All because her father had needed her. How many women would do such a thing?

As she collected her handbag and jacket,

Conall walked around to the passenger door to help her to the ground.

"I'll walk with you to the door," he told her. "Just in case your knees get spongy."

With his hand at her back, they walked through a sagging gate and down the rough walkway. To the east, far beyond the house, clouds had gathered over the Capitan Mountains, blotting out the sun and hinting at an oncoming rainstorm.

When they reached the porch, the goat ignored them as they stepped up to the door. "Would you like to come in?" she asked.

He smiled. "Some other time," he assured her. "If we're going to leave in the morning, I have a hundred things to tend to before we go. Richardson is coming about the pool at three. I need to be there to see what sort of ideas he has. And to get his estimates for the cost."

The idea of discussing plans to enlarge the swimming pool for Diamond D racehorses, while Vanessa was worrying how she was going to house two needy infants, made him feel rather small and out of touch. But it was hardly his fault that their worlds were so different.

"Sure," she said, then suddenly looked up at him. Her features were taut with stress. "Could you let me know about our flight time? Since my vehicle is still at the ranch, I suppose I'll need someone to pick me up and take me to the airport."

Placing his forefinger beneath her chin, he passed the pad of his thumb slowly along her jaw line. "Relax," he said softly. "I'll take care of everything, Vanessa. Just pack your bags and let me do the rest."

She nodded and then her gaze skittered shyly away from his and on to the closed door behind her shoulder. Conall told himself it was time to drop his hand and back away. But something about the tender line of her cheek, the warm scent emanating from her hair, made him bend his head and press a kiss to her temple.

For one moment her small hand fluttered to a stop against the middle of his chest, and then just as quickly she was pushing herself away and hurrying into the house.

Conall stared after her for long moments before he finally moved off the porch and walked back to his truck.

Later that evening, as Vanessa attempted to pack what things she needed for the trip to Vegas, the phone rang.

Praying it wasn't another call from Hope's

lawyer, she picked up the phone located on the nightstand by her bed and was surprised to hear Maura's voice on the other end of the line.

Even though the two women had been long-time friends, Maura had a husband and two young children to care for, along with her part-time job at Bridget's medical clinic in Ruidoso. She was too busy to make a habit of calling.

Without preamble, Conall's sister exclaimed, "Bridget just told me about your friend—and the babies! Dear God, I can't imagine what you must be feeling right now!"

Swiping a weary hand through her hair, Vanessa said, "I feel like every ounce of energy has been drained from my body, Maura."

"Bridget told me about you fainting. Thank God Conall was there with you. How are you feeling now?"

"Physically, better. I'm packing for the trip right now. But my mind is racing around in all directions. How can a person feel grief and happy excitement at the same time? I feel like I'm being pulled in all directions." She eased down on the edge of the bed. "But mostly, Maura, I'm scared."

"Scared? You?" Maura scoffed. "You're one of the strongest and bravest women I've ever known. What do you have to be scared about, anyway?"

Brave? Strong? Maybe at one time, years ago when she'd first headed out to Las Vegas on her own, she'd been brave and determined to make a better life for herself. But her mistakes with Jeff had wiped away much of her confidence.

"Two little infants, that's what! You've got to remember I've never had a baby. I don't know the first thing about taking care of one."

Maura's soft laugh was meant to reassure her friend. "Trust me, dear friend, giving birth doesn't give you an inside corner on taking care of babies. It's a learn-as-you-go thing. Believe me, you'll be fine. And isn't it wonderful, Vanna? You with children! You've wanted some of your own for so long now."

As tears stung, Vanessa squeezed her eyes shut. "That's true. But I didn't want them this way—with my friend dying. She was…well, I've talked about her to you before. She was such a generous person and so fun and full of life. She was planning to…come back here for a visit later this summer to show me the babies and see where I grew up. Now—" her throat tightened to an aching knot, forcing her to pause "—I'll be bringing the babies back without her."

Vanessa could hear Maura sniffing back a tear of her own. "Yes, it's so tragic, Vanna. I would have loved to meet her. But it wasn't meant to be and you can't dwell on her death now. You have to concentrate on the babies and remember how much your friend wanted them to be loved and cared for."

"You're right, Maura," Vanessa said as she tried to gather her ragged emotions. "I have to move forward now."

Maura cleared her throat. "Well, Bridget says that our brother is traveling with you to Vegas. Frankly, I'm shocked about this, Vanna. The rare times he leaves the ranch are only for business reasons."

Surely Maura could see that Conall considered Vanessa a business reason and nothing more. "I tried to tell him it wasn't necessary."

"Oh. I thought you might have asked him to go."

Vanessa drew in a sharp breath. "Are you serious? I would never ask Conall to do anything personal for me! He just made all these decisions on his own. And I have no idea why."

"Hmm. Well, his last secretary was a real bitch," Maura said bluntly. "And everyone in the family has heard him singing praises about your work. I'm sure he wants to keep you happy."

Vanessa released a short, dry laugh. "I've been told that good secretaries are hard to find." But earlier this afternoon, when he placed that brief kiss on the top of her head, she'd definitely not felt like his employee, she thought. She'd felt like a woman with something worthwhile to offer a man.

Dear God, the shock of losing Hope and becoming a mother all at once had numbed her brain. Conall Donovan would never look at her as anything more than his employee. Socially, he was several tiers above her. And even though he wasn't a snob, he was still a Donovan.

"Doesn't matter why he's going," Maura said. "I'm just glad he is. You need someone to support you at a time like this. And Conall has a strong arm to lean on."

Vanessa had no intentions of leaning on Conall. Certainly not in a physical way. But she kept those thoughts to herself. "Yes. Your brother is a rock."

"I wouldn't exactly call him that. Yes, he can be hard. But there's a soft side to him. You just have to know where to look for it," Maura explained. "There was a time—" She broke off, then after a long pause, added in a rueful voice, "Let's just say Conall wasn't always the man he is now."

Shying far away from that loaded comment, Vanessa said, "Well, I'm hoping we can wrap up everything in Vegas quickly."

"And I'd better let you go so that you can finish your packing," Maura replied. "Is there anything I can help you with while you're gone? Check on your father? Your house?"

"It's kind of you to offer, but I'll keep in touch with the nursing home. And I think the house will be okay for a couple of days. But just in case, you know where I leave an extra key so that you can get inside."

"Yes, I remember. In the little crack behind the window shutter."

"Right," Vanessa replied. "But I doubt we'll be gone for that long. Besides, the best thing you can do for me is share your experienced mothering skills. I'm definitely going to need advice."

Maura laughed. "Just wait, Vanna. You're going to see that a woman can never learn all there is to know about mothering. You just have to go by instinct and you happen to have a good one."

"I can only hope you're right," Vanessa murmured.

The next afternoon, after the short flight to Las Vegas, Conall dealt with their luggage, then picked up their rental car and headed to their hotel. Thankfully Fiona hadn't booked them into one of the resort monstrosities that lined the busy strip, but a nice peaceful villa on the desert outskirts of the city.

After checking in and sending their bags to adjoining rooms, they drove straight to the lawyer's office to deal with the legalities of claiming the twins and arranging to store Hope's ashes.

By the time they finally arrived at the orphanage, an old, ivy-covered Spanish-style building located on the outskirts of town, Vanessa's exhaustion must have been clearly showing. As they followed a silent Sister down a wide, empty corridor, Conall brought a steadying hand beneath her elbow.

"I'm thinking we should have waited until tomorrow to see the babies," he said in a low voice. "I'm not sure you're up to this."

Vanessa straightened her shoulders as best

she could. For the life of her, she wasn't about to let this granite piece of man think she was made of anything less than grit and determination.

"I'll be fine. And seeing the babies is the best part of this trip," she assured him.

Conall studied her pale face and wondered what his secretary could possibly be thinking. Even for the strongest of women, she was receiving a heavy load to carry. Especially without a man to help her.

He didn't know anything about Vanessa's marriage or divorce. In fact, he'd only known she was divorced because she'd stated it on her résumé. Of course he could have questioned Maura about her friend and most likely his sister would have given him an honest account of what had occurred. But Conall had never been one to pry into another person's private life, unless he believed there was a good reason to. He liked his privacy and tried his best to respect everyone else's. And even if she was his employee, he didn't consider Vanessa an exception to that rule. Except there were times, he had to admit to himself, that he was curious about her.

He gave her a wry smile. "To be honest, I'm looking forward to seeing them, too."

At the end of the corridor, the kindly nun ushered them into a sunny nursery filled with rows of cradles and cribs, all of them occupied with babies ranging from infancy to twelve months old. Three more nuns were moving quietly around the room, tending to the needy children, some of whom were crying boisterously.

"The twins are over here in the corner," the Sister said, motioning for the two of them to follow.

When she finally stopped near a pair of wooden cradles made of dark wood, she gestured toward the sleeping babies. Since the newborns were yet to be named, the two were differentiated with blue and pink blankets, while paper tags were attached to the end of each cradle, one reading Boy Valdez and the other Girl Valdez.

"Here they are," she announced. "Take as much time with them as you'd like. And if you need anything, please let me know. I'll be just down the hall in Mother Superior's office."

Conall and Vanessa both thanked the woman as she left and then they turned their entire attention to the sleeping twins.

Both babies had red-gold hair with the boy's being a slightly darker shade than his sister's.

To Conall, they appeared extremely tiny, even though the Sister had told them earlier that each baby weighed over five pounds, a fair amount for newborn twins.

"Oh. Oh, my. How...incredible," Vanessa whispered in awe as she stared down at the babies. "How perfectly beautiful!"

She bent over the cradles for a closer look and Conall watched as she touched a finger to the top of each velvety head. And then suddenly without warning, she covered her face with one hand and he could see her shoulders began to shake with silent sobs.

Quickly, he moved forward and wrapped an arm around her waist. "Vanessa." He said her name softly, just to remind her that she wasn't alone.

She glanced up at him, her brown eyes full of tears. "I'm sorry, Conall. I thought I could do this without breaking down. But... I—" Her gaze swung back to the babies. "I can't believe that I've been blessed with two beautiful babies. And yet I look at them and...can't help thinking of Hope."

His hand slipped to her slender shoulder and squeezed. "Your friend had the perfect name. Through you, she's given her children hope for the future. Remember that and smile."

She let out a ragged sigh. "You're right, Conall. I have to put my tears for Hope behind me and smile for the babies." Glancing up at him, she gave him a wobbly smile. "I've chosen names for them. Rose Marie and Richard Madison. What do you think?"

"Very nice. I'll call them Rose and Rick, if that's all right with you."

Her smile grew stronger. "That's my plan, too. Shall we pick them up?"

He stared at her, amazed that she wanted to include him. "We? You go ahead. I'm just an onlooker."

She looked a bit disappointed and Conall realized he felt a tad deflated himself. But whether that was because he actually wanted to hold the babies and was stupidly pretending indifference or because he was disheartening her at this special time, he didn't know.

Frowning, she asked, "You don't like babies or something?"

"Of course I do. I have baby nieces and nephews. But I didn't hold them when they were this small. Come to think of it...none of them were ever this small." He gestured toward the twins. "I might do it all wrong."

"I might do it all wrong, too," she suggested. "So we might as well try together."

Realizing it would look strange if he kept protesting, he said, "All right. I'll watch you first."

She bent over Rose's cradle and after carefully placing a hand beneath the baby's head, lifted her out of the bed and into her arms. After a moment, Conall moved up to the other cradle and, in the same cautious manner, reached for the boy.

Once he had the child safely positioned in the crook of his arm, he adjusted the thin blue blanket beneath little Rick's chin so that he could get a better look at his face. It was perfectly formed with a little pug nose and bow-shaped lips. Faint golden brows framed a set of blue eyes that were now wide open and appeared to be searching to see who or what was holding him.

Vulnerable. Needy. Precious. As he held the child, memories carried him back to when he and Nancy had first married. In the beginning, he'd had so many dreams and plans. All of them surrounding a house full of children to carry on the Donovan name and inherit the hard-earned rewards of the Diamond D. But those dreams had slowly and surely come crashing down.

Now as Conall experienced the special

warmth and scent of the baby boy lying so helplessly in the crook of his arm, Conall wasn't sure that Vanessa yet realized what a treasure she'd been handed. But he did. Oh, how he did.

"Conall?"

Reining in his thoughts, he pulled his gaze away from the baby to find her staring at him with a faintly puzzled look on her face. Had she been reading his mind? Conall wondered. Surely not. Down through the years he'd perfected the art of shuttering his emotions. Baby Rick wasn't strong enough to make him change the longtime habit.

"Am I doing something wrong?" he asked.

For the first time Conall could remember, his secretary actually smiled at him with those big brown eyes of hers.

"No. You look like you were tailor-made for the job of Daddy."

Her observation struck him hard, but he did his best to keep the pain hidden, as though there was no wide, empty hole inside him.

"Not hardly," he said gruffly. "I'm not... daddy material."

One delicate brow arched skeptically upward. "Oh? You don't ever plan to have children of your own?"

For some reason her question made him pull the baby boy even closer to his chest. "That's one thing I'm absolutely certain I'll never have."

Clearly taken aback by his response, her gaze slipped away from his and dropped to the baby in her arms. "Well, everyone has their own ideas about having children," she said a bit stiffly. "I just happen to think you're making a sad mistake."

A sad mistake. Oh, yes, it was a sad mistake that she was misjudging him, Conall thought. And sad, too, that he couldn't find the courage to tell this woman that at one time he'd planned to have at least a half-dozen children.

But if he let her in on that dream, then he'd have to explain why he'd been forced to set it aside. And why he planned to live the rest of his life a lone bachelor.

Hardening himself to that certain reality had changed him, he knew. Even his family often considered him unapproachable. But none of them actually understood the loss he felt to see his siblings having children of their own, while knowing he would always be cheated out of one of life's most blessed gifts.

"You have a right to your opinion, Vanessa.

Just like I have a right to live my life the way I see fit."

She cast him a pained look, then turned her back to him and walked a few steps away as though she'd just seen him for the first time and didn't like what she was seeing.

Well, that was okay, Conall thought. What his secretary thought about him didn't matter. It wasn't as if they were romantically linked, or even close friends.

He looked down at the baby in his arms and felt something raw and sweet swell in his chest. Vanessa would no doubt provide the twins with love. But they needed a father. And at some point in the future she would probably provide them with one. Then her family circle would be complete and that was only right.

Yet strangely, the idea left Conall with a regretful ache.

Chapter Three

Later that evening, long after their visit to the orphanage had ended, Vanessa sat in a quiet courtyard behind their villa-style hotel, and tried to relax from the hectic pace of the day. Along with the busy schedule of flying, meeting with lawyers and visiting the babies, her cell phone had rung continually all afternoon. Most of the calls were from people here in Vegas who'd been mutual friends of her and Hope and were just now hearing about the tragedy. Vanessa appreciated their concern and interest, but she was exhausted from explaining about the twins and sharing her grief over Hope's death.

Finally, in desperation, she'd left the phone in her room and walked outside to enjoy the cooling desert air. Now as she sat on an iron bench beneath a huge Joshua tree and watched darkness fall on the distant mountains, she wished she could turn off thoughts of Conall as easily as she'd turned off the phone.

The man was an enigma. After weeks of working with him, she still didn't understand what made Conall tick or what drove him to work long, trying hours for the ranch. Clearly he was ambitious. Every morning he arrived at the office at least two hours ahead of her, which meant he went to work before daylight. And when she left in the evenings, even after working overtime herself, he remained at his desk making calls or meeting with horse-racing connections. Running the Diamond D was clearly more than a job to him. It was the entire sum of his life. Did he invest so much of himself because the ranch was family owned and operated?

She could only guess at the answer to that question. But there was no doubt that Conall was a man of striking looks with plenty of money to match. The ranch could easily afford to hire an assistant in order to free Conall from his grueling schedule. With part of his workload eased, he'd be able to travel the world and indulge in all sorts of lavish recreations, with a trail of willing women trotting behind him. Yet none of those things appeared to interest him in the least. She seriously doubted he would accept the help of an assistant, even if the person volunteered to work for free. He was a man who wanted things done his way and refused to trust just anyone to carry out his orders.

Vanessa often wondered if he was still bitter over his divorce, or perhaps he was still in love with his ex-wife and wanted her back. Maura had never mentioned the cause of her brother's divorce and Vanessa wasn't about to question her childhood friend about him. The hopes and dreams and feelings going on inside Conall weren't her business. Or so she kept telling herself. But ever since she'd looked up in the orphanage and seen him standing there with her baby son in his arms, she'd been consumed with unexpected emotions and questions.

The fact that he didn't want or expect to ever have children had shaken her deeply. Of all the men she'd met through the years, Conall had always seemed like a man who would love and welcome children into his life. True, he had a dark and dangerous appearance but it belied the responsible man beneath. He wasn't a roamer or playboy with a wild lifestyle. Why would he not want children? Because there was no room in his heart for them? No. Vanessa couldn't believe he was that cold or stingy with himself. Not after seeing the way he interacted with the twins.

"Vanessa?"

The unexpected sound of Conall's voice had her glancing over her shoulder to see him walking a narrow brick pathway toward her. Figuring something had to be wrong for him to come all the way out here to find her, she rose from the bench and met him on the footpath.

"I'm sorry," she quickly apologized. "I left my phone in the room. Has the lawyer or orphanage been trying to reach me?"

Impatience creased his forehead. "You need to quit all this worrying, Vanessa. No one has tried to reach you through me. The lawyer seemed very competent. I'm sure he'll have the last of the papers for us to sign before we catch our flight out tomorrow afternoon. And from what Mother Superior told us, the babies are perfectly healthy and able to travel."

Shaking her head, Vanessa forced the tenseness in her shoulders to relax. "I am a bit on edge," she admitted. "My phone has been ringing all evening and—"

Before she could finish, the cell in his shirt pocket went off and after a quick glance at the caller ID he said, "Sorry, Vanessa, I've been having the same problem. This won't take but a minute or two."

With a quick nod, she turned her back and took a few steps away to where water trickled over a three-tiered fountain and into a small pool. As she watched colorful koi swim in and out of water plants, she heard him say, "No. That won't do....I understand you mean well. But nothing used....Everything new....Yes, classic....No. Something like cherry and antique....Got it?... Yeah. And anything else you can think of that will be needed." There was a long pause as he listened to the caller and then he replied. "Yeah. Thanks, sis....Good night."

His sister? That could be Maura, Dallas or Bridget, she thought. Apparently they were planning something together and the notion sent a sad pang through Vanessa. She'd never had a sister to conspire with and share experiences, only older brothers who'd mostly caused great agony for her parents. Now with Esther, her mother, gone and her father, Alonzo, still having trouble communicating with his halting speech, she couldn't look for family support. Unlike Conall, who'd always been surrounded by loving siblings, parents and grandmother.

"Well, now that I have that out of the way," Conall announced behind her, "I came out here to see if you'd like to go to dinner somewhere? We've not eaten in hours."

Vanessa glanced down at herself. She was still wearing the simple pink sheathe she'd started out with this morning, minus the matching bolero sweater, but it was wrinkled and even without the aid of a mirror she knew her hair was blown to a tumbled mess. "I really don't feel like dressing up for dinner, Conall. You go on without me."

He chuckled and the sound took her by surprise. He was a man who rarely laughed and when he did it was usually about something that she didn't find amusing. Now as she looked at him, she was jarred by his jovial attitude.

"Have you taken a look at me?" he asked. "I'm wearing jeans."

Dragging her gaze away from the charming grin on his lips, she slowly inspected the blue denim encasing his muscled thighs and the pair of brown alligator boots he wore. He was one of those few men who looked comfortable dressed up or down, which meant he would probably look even better without any clothes at all.

Dear, God, what was she doing? Now wasn't the time for those sorts of indecent thoughts, she scolded herself. As far as Conall went, there would never be a time for them. And she had more important issues to focus on. Like two little tots with golden-red hair and blue eyes.

"I am hungry," she admitted. For food. Not for a man like him, she mentally added.

"Great. There's a little restaurant right across the street that looks good."

"Just give me a moment to fetch my purse and sweater from the room," she told him.

A few minutes later, they were seated at a small table in a family-type restaurant that featured Italian dishes. Vanessa ordered ravioli while Conall chose steak and pasta. As they waited for their salads and drinks to be served, Conall glanced around the long room decorated with early dated photos of Las Vegas and simple, home-style tables covered in brightly striped cloths.

Seated directly across from him, Vanessa asked, "Is this place not to your liking? We can always find another restaurant."

Surprised by her suggestion, he turned his gaze on her. "I'm perfectly satisfied. Why do you ask?"

One of her slender shoulders lifted and fell in a negligible way. "I don't know. The way you were looking around and frowning."

"I frown all the time." A wry smile touched one corner of his mouth. "At least, that's what my mother tells me."

"Mothers don't like to see their children frown," she reasoned. "Mine never did. She always told me to smile and count my blessings."

As Conall's gaze dwelled on his secretary's face, he was surprised at how easy and pleasurable it was to look at her and be in her company. He'd not expected to enjoy any part of this trip. He'd only done it because she was a woman alone and in need, and she was a dedicated employee. But he was quickly discovering that Vanessa was more than an efficient secretary, she was a lovely woman and, like it or not, desire was beginning to stir in him for the first time in a long, long time.

"You must miss your mother terribly," he said. "I was surprised when I heard about her passing. The last time I'd seen her in church she seemed very spry."

Her gaze suddenly dropped to the tabletop, but Conall didn't miss the sadness on her face. The image bothered him almost as much as her tears had yesterday. And for some reason he felt guilty for not attending Mrs. Valdez's funeral services. Even though he'd not known the woman personally, he should have made the effort for Vanessa's sake. But at that time, she'd not been working as his secretary; she'd merely been a past acquaintance, who'd left the valley years ago.

"Yes. Mama appeared to be a picture of health. That made her sudden heart attack even harder to take," she said quietly, then lifted her gaze back to him. "Her death was one of the main reasons I left Las Vegas and returned to Tinnie. I missed the end of my mother's life. I want to be around for my father as much as I can before…he leaves me."

Other than the twins, she certainly didn't have much in the way of family. The idea troubled Conall, although he wasn't sure why. Plenty of people he knew had lost their parents or were lacking family of any kind and they didn't necessarily garner his sympathy. At least, not the deep sort of regret he felt for Vanessa.

"You gave up a very good job to return to

your family home and your father," he commented. "I have to admire you for that, Vanessa."

Her eyes were full of doubt as they connected with his.

"I'm not sure that I made the most sensible decision, Conall. I did have a good job and a little house in a nice part of town. Materially speaking, I had much more here in Vegas than I ever had in the valley. But..." Pausing, she let out a long sigh. "Money isn't a cure-all."

No one knew that any better than Conall. Money couldn't change the fact that a childhood fever had killed his chances to ever father a child of his own. Nor had money been able to fix his shattered marriage. In fact, being rich had only compounded the problems he'd endured with Nancy. But since his divorce he'd tried his best to bury those painful personal details. They certainly weren't matters he wanted to discuss with a woman, and that included Vanessa.

"You're not worried about the twins' financial future, are you?" he asked. "Hope's life insurance appears to have left them set up nicely for college."

"I'm not worried about the financial part of

this," she replied. "My parents raised six children. Surely I can manage two."

"But you're not married," he pointed out.

From the stiff line of her shoulders to the purse of her lips, everything about her looked offended by his comment.

"You think having a man around would be a help?"

The bitterness in her short laugh was something he'd never heard from her before. The idea that this gentle woman might hold any sort of hard streak inside her took him by surprise. "I'm a man," he answered. "I like to think we're a helpful gender."

Frowning, her gaze left his to travel to an insignificant spot across the room. "Look, Conall, I've already had one husband I had to support, I don't want another. I can do just fine without that added burden."

So she'd ended up marrying a man just like her parasitic brothers. No wonder there was bitterness on her tongue. But how and why had she made such a mistake in judgment? He would have thought she'd seen enough freeloading men to spot one at first glance.

Yeah. Just like you'd been able to spot Nancy's twisted character. You didn't use good judgment with her, either. You allowed love to lead you around. And around. Until you were walking down a path of destruction.

Clearing his throat, he tried to ignore the mocking voice going off inside him. "I wasn't trying to suggest—"

Shaking her head, she interrupted, "Forget it, please. I...didn't mean to sound so catty. It's just that after Jeff... Well, I resent the idea of being told I need a man."

Like he resented his family telling him he needed another woman in his life, Conall thought. Hell, getting hooked up with another woman like Nancy would finish him. And finding a nice, family-oriented woman that he could love wasn't as simple as it sounded. Oh, he'd tried. Once the initial blow of his divorce was over, he'd returned to the dating scene and attempted to put his heart into starting his life over with another woman. But as soon as he made it clear that he couldn't father children, all his dates had backed away from him. Sure, for the most part they'd all been kind and empathetic to his problem, but in the end none of them had wanted to start out their lives with a man that couldn't give them a family of their own. After a while, Conall had grown so weary of being rejected over and over that he'd finally given up on finding love, marriage and anything in between. And for the past few years he'd pretty much convinced himself that he was better off being alone and focusing all his attention to his job.

Vanessa's cynical remark was still dangling in the air between them when the waitress arrived with their drinks and salads. After the young woman served them and went on her way, he could feel Vanessa's gaze on him and he paused from the task of stirring sugar into his tea to glance at her. Clearly, from the expression on her face, she wanted to speak her mind about something.

"What?" he prompted.

She hesitated before giving her head a slight shake. The gentle waves of hair lying on her shoulders shook with the movement as did the blue teardrops dangling from her earlobes. Suddenly Conall was wondering how it would feel to thrust his fingers into her silky hair, to nibble on the perfect little shell of her ear.

"I don't know how to say this, Conall, without making you angry."

Trying to concentrate on her words instead of the erotic images in his mind, he asked, "What makes you think I'll be angry? I've not gotten angry with you yet, have I?"

He would admit that he often got frustrated

with business dealings and the roadblocks he
encountered while dealing with the multitudes
of details that went into managing a ranch the
size of the Diamond D. But he'd never gotten
upset with Vanessa. She'd always given more
than a hundred percent to her job and he appreciated her effort.

She reached for the pepper shaker and shook
it vigorously over her salad. "Because you're
going to think I'm ungrateful. And I'm not.
I'm actually very indebted to you for making
this trip with me and…everything else you've
taken care of. But I—"

A faint smile curled up one corner of his
mouth.

"You don't want me telling you how to take
care of the twins or what you might need in
your personal life. Is that it?"

She studied him for a long moment and then
laughed softly under her breath. Conall likened
the sound to sweet music.

"That's about it," she answered.

Amused by her streak of independence, he
finished stirring his tea. "In other words, while
we're on this trip I need to forget that I'm your
boss and you're my secretary."

The tip of her tongue came out to moisten
her lips and Conall found himself gazing at

the damp sheen it left behind. What would she taste like? he wondered. Honey? Wine? Or simply all woman? He certainly didn't need to know. But he sure as hell wouldn't mind making the effort to find out.

She said, "Uh, well, I suppose that's a way of putting it."

The smile on his face deepened and he realized with a start that he was flirting. Something he'd not done in years or, for that matter, even wanted to do.

"Good," he said.

One of her winged brows shot upward. "Good? I thought you were a man who always wanted to be the boss."

Chuckling softly, he reached across the table and enfolded her small hand with his. "Not tonight. I'd rather just be a man having dinner with a beautiful woman. What do you think about that?"

She grimaced, but he could see a faint swathe of pink rushing over her cheeks and her breasts rising and falling with each quick intake of breath. The notion that he was affecting her, even in this small way, was like a heady drink of wine to him, and in the far back of his mind, he wondered what was coming over him. Clearly he wasn't himself. He'd not been himself since yesterday when he'd walked through the office and found Vanessa with tears on her cheeks.

"I think there's something about this town that makes people forget who and what they are. But I never thought you'd be the type to fall prey to its lure," she said dryly. "The next thing I know you'll be saying we should take a stroll down the strip and take in the lights."

"Hmm. That's a great idea. We'll go as soon as we finish eating."

Less than an hour later, after the two of them found a parking space and made their way to the busy sidewalks lining the city's most famous boulevard, Vanessa was still wishing she'd kept her mouth shut. Spending time with Conall away from the office was something she'd often dreamed about, but she was smart enough to realize it was risky business.

In spite of what he'd said back at the restaurant, he was her boss and she depended on him for her livelihood. Allowing herself to think of him as anything more than the man who signed her paychecks would be like inviting trouble right through the front door. Yet here she was walking close to his side and enjoying every second of it.

"Is this the first time you've ever visited Las Vegas?" Vanessa asked as they slowly made their way southward along the busy sidewalk running adjacent to the congested street.

"No. Believe it or not, I was here once with my parents. We'd gone out to Santa Anita to watch one of our horses run in a graded stakes race. On the way back Mom wanted to stop off and play the slots. So Dad and I endured while she had fun."

The night had cooled to a balmy temperature and as the light wind caressed her face, Vanessa realized this was the first time she'd relaxed since she'd gotten the call from Hope's lawyer.

"You don't like to gamble?" she asked.

"Not that much."

She smiled with amused disbelief. "How can you say that, Conall? You're in the racehorse business. That's a big, big gamble."

He chuckled. "That's true. But in my business I pretty much know what I'm investing in. At least I can see my venture and put my hands on it." He gestured to one of the massive casinos to their right. "In there you're placing your money on pure chance."

"Like the stock market," she joked.

"Exactly," he said with another short laugh,

then added, "I didn't realize you could be a funny girl."

"I have my moments."

She was thinking what a nice deep laugh he had and how much she enjoyed hearing it when his arm suddenly slid around the back of her waist and drew her even closer to his side. The sudden contact nearly took her breath, yet she did her best to hide the havoc he was causing inside her. After all, she wasn't that same teenager who'd had such a crush on him so many years ago. She'd grown up, dated, married and divorced. Men weren't a big deal to her anymore. Or so she'd believed. Until tonight. When Conall had suddenly started to treat her like a woman instead of a secretary.

"Even though it's not my cup of tea, I have to admit there's something magical about this town. Do you miss all this?" he asked, as he gestured toward the elaborately designed buildings, the endless lights and the bumper-to-bumper traffic on the strip.

"No. I never was into the bright lights and glamour of this place. I only saw it as a town of opportunities. And I took them. Before I ever left the valley, I decided if I had to work my way through college waitressing, I might as well do it where I could make the most money."

"I certainly don't blame you for that."

No. He wouldn't, Vanessa thought. He was the sort of person who never looked down on anyone because they had less than him. And he admired any person who worked hard for a living.

Conall gestured to an area several feet away where a low curved wall contained a shallow pool with spraying spouts of water. "Let's take a rest over there by the pool," he suggested.

"Sounds good to me," she agreed.

Beneath a huge palm tree they took seats on the wide concrete wall. As the two of them made themselves comfortable, he dropped his arm from her waist and Vanessa was trying to decide if she was relieved or disappointed at the loss of contact, when he reached for her hand and folded it casually within his.

Staring out at the street of heavy traffic and gawking pedestrians, Conall grunted with dismay. "After working in this town, the Diamond D must seem mundane."

"The Diamond D is a busy place, too," she disagreed. "Only in a different way."

The idea that his thigh was pressed slightly against hers and that the heat from his hand was radiating all the way up to her shoulder was making every nerve inside Vanessa tighten to the screaming point. Why was he getting this close to her? She'd worked for the man for more than two months and he'd never touched her in any form or fashion until yesterday when she'd fainted straight into his arms. Now he was behaving as though he had every right to put his arm around her or hold her hand.

If she had any sense at all, she'd put a stop to it, Vanessa argued with herself. She'd tell him to keep his hands to himself and remember that she was his secretary and nothing more. But she'd already made the foolish mistake of telling him to forget about being her boss while they were here in Vegas. And she'd be lying to herself, and to him, if she tried to say she wasn't enjoying the feel of his warm fingers wrapped so snugly around hers.

Clearing her throat, she said, "I have to confess that when I first returned to Lincoln County, I did so with intentions of getting a job at the Billy the Kid Casino. I have a friend there who works in the business office and he would have given me a glowing reference. But I'd already worked in that industry for so long that I thought a complete change might be good for me. And then I read about your job opening and I…" She paused long enough to give him a wry smile. "I almost didn't call you."

One of his black brows lifted slightly and as her gaze wandered over his cool gray eyes and dark profile, she felt her heart thud into a rhythm that actually scared her. The man wasn't supposed to be making her feel light-headed. He wasn't supposed to be making her forget they were hundreds of miles away from the office or reminding her they were in a town that urged people to be a little reckless.

"Why?" he asked. "You didn't think you'd like working for me?"

"That wasn't the reason. I didn't want you giving me the job just because I was Maura's old friend. But I should have known you were the type of man who'd never put sentimentality over business. You'd never be that easy with…anyone."

Suddenly his expression turned solemn and Vanessa felt her heart kick to an even faster rate.

"If it makes you feel any better, Vanessa, I can assure you that you got the job on your own merit. Not through a friendship with my sister."

She nervously licked her lips and wondered why she couldn't tear her eyes away from his rugged face. All around her there were fabulous sights that should be monopolizing her attention. But none of them, she realized, could compete with Conall.

"I'm glad you told me," she said, her voice dropping to a husky note.

"And are you glad you took the job?"

How could she answer that without incriminating herself? This man had no idea that he was the thing that fueled her, pushed her out of bed in the morning and made her want to hope and dream again, even after she'd thought her future had died.

"So far," she said lowly. "What about you? Do you wish you'd offered it to someone else?"

A sexy grin suddenly exposed his white teeth and Vanessa was mesmerized by the sight. She'd never seen this side of him before and the notion that he was showing it to her was almost more than she could take in.

"Giving you the job was one of the smartest decisions I've ever made." Leaning closer, he gently pushed his fingers into her windblown hair and smoothed it away from her cheek. "And coming on this trip with you was even smarter."

By now her breathing was coming in shallow sips and she had to swallow before she could finally form one word. "Why?"

His head drew so close to hers that she could see little more than his mouth and nose.

"Because it's opened my eyes. And I'm beginning to see all the things I've been missing."

"Conall." His name passed her lips as she hesitantly pressed a hand against his chest. "This…you… I don't understand."

"That makes two of us."

"But we—"

"Don't talk," he whispered. "Talking won't change the fact that I want to kiss you."

Even if she could have said another word, she doubted it would have stopped what he was about to do. What *she* was about to do.

His thumb and forefinger closed around her chin and then his lips settled over hers. Vanessa closed her eyes and for the first time in a long time, she stopped thinking and simply let herself feel.

Chapter Four

The desert wind teased her hair and brushed her skin, but it did little to ease the heat building inside Vanessa. Conall's mouth was like a flame licking, consuming, turning her whole body to liquid fire.

Beyond them she could hear the movement of the crawling traffic and among the nearby pedestrians, the occasional burst of conversation punctuated with laughter. Above their heads, the fans of the palm trees whipped noisily in the wind. Yet none of these distractions were enough to jerk Vanessa back to sanity.

Instead, she simply wanted to sit there forever, tasting his mouth, feeling his hands move against her skin. This wasn't the same as the fantasies she'd had of Conall while they'd been teenagers. This was very, very real and so was the effect it was having on her body.

She was melting into him, her senses totally absorbed with his kiss when somewhere behind them voices called out loudly. The interruption broke the connection of their lips and Conall finally lifted his head to gaze down at her.

What could she possibly say to him now? she wondered. Or should she even try?

He cleared his throat and she suddenly realized his hand was cupped against the side of her face. The skin of his palm was rough and raspy, yet his touch was as gentle as a dove's. She wanted to rub her cheek against the masculine texture, experience the erotic friction.

"I guess we'd better be moving along," he said huskily. "Or I...might start forgetting we're in a public place."

Start forgetting? Vanessa had forgotten their whereabouts a long time ago. Like the first moment his lips had touched hers! The idea that she'd become so lost and reckless in his arms was downright terrifying. She couldn't afford to get entangled in an affair with this man. He had the power to hurt her emotionally, not to mention the right to terminate her job whenever the whim hit him.

Trying to put her focus on her new babies, rather than the growing need in her hungry body, she turned and scooted several generous inches away from him.

"I think you're right." Her voice was raw and awkward, but that was better than appearing totally speechless, she thought with a bit of desperation. "And it's getting late. I think we should head back to the hotel."

Apparently he agreed, because he took her by the arm and helped her up from the low concrete wall. Without exchanging any more words, he guided her back onto the busy sidewalk and in the general direction of their rental car.

Close to ten minutes passed before he finally spoke and by then Vanessa had decided he was going to totally ignore what had happened. No doubt he was regretting giving in to the impulse of kissing his secretary. Especially kissing her as though he was enjoying every moment their lips had been locked together.

Oh, God, what had she done? What was he thinking now? That she was easy and gullible and helpless? That she was so stupid she'd allowed his kiss to go to her head and her heart?

"I hope you're not angry with me, Vanessa."

Stunned by this statement, she glanced his way. "I'm not angry. Why should I be?"

He stared up ahead of them and she could see they had reached the parking area where they'd left the car.

He answered, "Because I wasn't behaving like myself back there. Because I shouldn't have taken advantage of the moment like that. You've been through a lot these past couple of days."

So it hadn't really been him kissing her back there, she thought dismally, just a part of him that had succumbed to impulse. Well, that shouldn't surprise her. Conall was normally a calculated man and under normal circumstances he would never plan to make a pass at her. The notion bothered her far more than it should have.

"I'm a big girl. I could have pushed you away."

"Yeah, but—"

She groaned. "Let's forget the kiss, Conall."

"I don't want to forget it. I want to repeat it."

That was enough to stop her in her tracks and she looked at him with faint amazement.

She mumbled, "That's not going to happen."

He moved closer and when his hand came

to rest on her shoulder, she felt herself melting all over again.

"Why?" he asked. "Because you liked it?"

Deciding now was the perfect time to be totally honest, she answered, "Yes. And to let anything start brewing between us now would be a big mistake."

A deep furrow appeared between his black brows. "Maybe you're right," he murmured, then before she could make any sort of reply, he placed a hand at her back and ushered her on toward the car. "But I'm not totally convinced that you are. Yet."

A shiver of uncertain anticipation rolled down Vanessa's spine. From now on she was going to have to stay on guard whenever she was with this man. Otherwise, she might wake up and find herself in his bed.

The next morning as Vanessa stepped out of the shower and slipped into a satin robe, a knock sounded on the door. Knowing it was far too early for housekeeping, she glanced through the peephole to see Conall standing on the opposite side of the door.

The sight of him surprised her. It wasn't quite seven yet. Last night when they'd returned to the hotel and parted ways, he'd not mentioned anything about meeting this early.

"It's me, Vanessa."

Drawing in a bracing breath, she opened the door and stared at him. He was already dressed in a pair of dark, Western-cut slacks and a crisp white shirt. His deep brown hair was combed back from his face and there was a faint smile on his lips, a soft sort of expression that she'd never seen on him before.

Her heart beating fast and hard, she blurted, "I'm not dressed yet."

His gray gaze slowly left her face to slide all the way to her bare toes. Vanessa had never felt so exposed in her life.

"I wasn't planning on us going out just yet," he explained. "I wanted to talk with you. Before we left the hotel."

Knowing she would look childish and prudish to send him away, she pulled the door wider and gestured for him to enter her room.

As he stepped past her, she clutched the front of her robe to her breasts and hoped he didn't notice the naked shape of them beneath the clinging fabric.

"Is something wrong?" she asked as she shut the door after him.

"No. And why do you always suspect something is wrong whenever I show up? You act like I'm some sort of bearer of bad news."

Her cheeks warmed with color as she joined him in the middle of the room. "I just…wasn't expecting you to be out so early. That's all. And all this legal stuff with the babies is not like anything I've dealt with before. I'll be glad when I sign the final documents this morning, before anything can go wrong."

"Nothing is going to go wrong," he said gently, "and the babies are what I'm here to talk to you about."

She stared at him, her brows lifted in question. "What else is there to talk about?"

Vanessa saw his eyes slide to the king-sized bed. The covers were rumpled and she'd left a set of black lacy lingerie lying atop the white sheet. She wondered what he was thinking. Was he remembering the kiss they'd shared last night or the intimate times he'd shared with his ex-wife?

"A few things," he said pensively, then focused his gaze back on her face. "I'll call room service for breakfast and we can eat out on the patio while we talk."

It was a statement, not a question, and for a moment she bristled at his authoritative attitude. She wanted to remind him that they were in a hotel room—her room to be exact—and he was supposed to be behaving as a supportive friend, not a boss. But she kept the thoughts to herself. Asking him to forget he was her boss while they were here in Vegas had already caused problems. Now wasn't the time or place to take that risk again.

"All right," she told him. "While you call I'll get dressed."

Crossing to the bed, she snatched up her lingerie, then walked to the closet to take down her dress. Behind her, she heard him picking up the phone.

"What would you like?" he called to her. "Fresh fruit and yogurt?"

Frowning, she turned to look at him. "You mean I get to order for myself?"

A sheepish smile settled over his face and that was all it took to turn her insides to mushy oatmeal.

"Sorry, Vanessa. I don't mean to be bossy but it—"

"Just comes natural to you," she finished with an understanding smile. "I'll bet you always tried to tell your younger siblings what to do and how to do it."

He laughed. "Somebody had to."

This was not the Conall she'd been working

for the past two months, Vanessa thought. This man was far more approachable and endearing. He was also far more dangerous.

"Well, I do like fresh fruit and yogurt, but I need something more substantial this morning. Make it bacon and eggs and wheat toast."

"A woman who likes to eat in the morning. I like that," he said.

She was afraid to ask what he meant by that remark, so she simply excused herself and hurried to the bathroom to dress.

By the time she'd finished pulling on her clothes, swiping on a bit of makeup and combing her hair into casual waves around her face, she heard room service arriving.

She stepped from the bathroom just as Conall was handing the server a hefty tip. As the young man headed out the door, he turned to Vanessa.

"Everything is waiting out on the patio," he announced.

"Great. I'm starving."

Outside the morning was perfect with a blue, blue sky and a warm, gentle breeze. The table holding their breakfast was situated on a red brick patio edged by a row of palm trees. Thick blooming shrubs and tall agave plants acted as a privacy fence between the rooms. As Conall helped her into one of the rattan chairs, Vanessa couldn't help thinking the villa would be a perfect place for a honeymoon.

A honeymoon, she thought wryly. That kiss Conall had given her last night had messed up her thinking and had her dreaming about things she had no business dreaming about. She'd had her chance at love and marriage. It hadn't worked. And now she seriously doubted she'd ever find a man who would truly love her. A man she could trust with all her heart.

"I'm sure you've been wondering what I wanted to speak with you about," he said as the two of them began to eat.

Vanessa fortified herself with a long sip of strong coffee as she watched him slather a piece of toast with apricot jam.

"I am curious," she admitted.

"I've been thinking about your housing situation," he said before he bit into the toast.

"What is there to think about? I have my parents' home."

"Yes. But there's a house on the ranch that was vacated only a few days ago. It was just remodeled only last year with new flooring and up-to-date appliances. You'd have plenty of room for yourself and a nursery. And you'd be on the ranch—close by—in case you needed help."

Stunned and just a little vexed, Vanessa looked at him. "You know what my salary is, Conall. I couldn't afford to lease the house."

"Why not? It wouldn't cost you a penny."

All she could do was stare at him. "It's obvious you don't know me, Conall. Otherwise, you'd know that I don't go around looking for, or expecting, handouts."

He leveled a frustrated frown at her. "If you think I'm making you a *special* offer because you're my secretary, then you're in for a surprise. Not all of our employees are housed on the ranch and that's fine, too. But the housing we do supply for our ranch hands and house staff is considered a part of their salary, one of the benefits for working for the Diamond D. As I see it, you are an employee and the house is there—empty for now—but I can assure you, not for long."

Vanessa felt more than a little embarrassed. She'd quickly jumped to the conclusion that he was offering her an exclusive deal. All because he'd made this trip with her and given her that one long, mind-shattering kiss. How foolish could she be? He was a man who liked to help people whenever the opportunity arose. And he'd apparently enjoyed that kiss he'd given her. He'd said he wanted to repeat it. But in spite of that pleasant physical exchange, Conall Donovan didn't view her as anything special. She was simply his secretary.

"I'm sorry, Conall. Since the general-managing office handles that sort of thing I wasn't aware that the Diamond D offered housing to its employees free of charge."

A faint smile touched his lips as his gaze slid curiously over her face and Vanessa wondered how a pair of gray eyes could look so warm or how their gaze could feel even hotter to her skin.

"I see. So does that change your mind about moving to the ranch? I'd certainly feel a lot better about you and babies knowing you had close neighbors."

Up to a point, she could understand his thinking. Her parents' home was fairly isolated, with the nearest neighbor being a good five miles away. And even though the Valdezes' had raised five children in the tiny stucco structure, the rooms were small and limited to what she could do with them.

Still, the home was hers now and she was proud of it. She didn't need the best of things to be happy and that's the way she wanted her

twins to be raised—without the need for material trappings. He ought to understand that.
He ought to know that for him to merely imply
she needed to find some place "better" was of-
fensive and hurtful to her. Besides, after dealing with Jeff, she wanted her independence.
Needed it, in fact. But she didn't want to go
into that now with Conall.

Reaching for the insulated coffeepot, she
added a splash of the hot liquid to her cooling cup. "I thank you for the offer. But, no. It
doesn't change my mind. Until I get the hang
of it, taking care of two newborns is going to
be…well, challenging. I need to be in a place
where I feel comfortable and at home. And
that's at my own place." Her gaze met his. "I
hope you understand."

Conall dropped his attention to his plate as
he shoveled up a forkful of egg and wondered
why he felt so disappointed. It wasn't as if he
was a green teenager and she'd turned him
down for a date. Last night, after he'd left her
at the door of her room, the idea of offering her
housing had entered his mind and once he'd
gone to bed, he'd lain awake for some time
imagining how it would be to have her and her
new little family close by. He'd liked the idea
so much that he'd rushed over here early to tell

her about it. Now, seeing how she didn't want his help, he felt deflated and foolish.

"I understand that you women have your own ideas about things," he said. "I can accept that."

Even though her sigh was barely discernible, he heard it. The sound put a faint frown between his brows as he wondered why anything she was thinking and feeling about him should matter. Hell, she was just his secretary. Just because she'd become the sudden mother of twin infants didn't make her any different than the woman who'd worked in his office for the past two months, he reasoned with himself.

Yet this whole thing with the babies had forced Conall to see Vanessa in a more personal way. And last night, when he'd succumbed to his urges and kissed her, something had clicked inside him. Suddenly he'd been feeling, wanting, needing. All at once he'd felt the dead parts of him waking and bursting to life again.

Conall realized it was stupid of him to hang so much importance on one kiss. But he couldn't put it or her out of his mind.

"I'm glad," she said, "because I don't want to appear ungrateful."

He smiled at her. "Good. Because I have another offer for you. Especially since you turned the last one down," he added.

Her brows lifted with faint curiosity and Conall couldn't help but notice how the early morning sun was kissing her pearly skin and bathing it with a golden sheen. Last night, when he'd touched her face and laid his cheek against hers, he'd been overwhelmed at the softness and even now a part of him longed to reach across the table and trail his fingers across her skin, her lips.

"Don't you think you've already offered me enough?" she asked dryly.

Reaching for his coffee, he tried to sound like he was discussing business with a client. "Not yet. This is something essential to you and to me. I don't want to lose you as a secretary, so while you're at work you're going to need child care services. I insist that the ranch provide you with a nanny. Two, if need be."

She fell back against her chair and Conall could see he'd shocked her. Clearly, she'd not been expecting him to offer her any sort of amenities simply because she was a Diamond D employee. In fact, she acted as though it would be wrong for her to accept anything from him. Which was quite a contrast to his ex-wife, who'd grabbed and snatched anything and everything she could, then expected more.

"Don't you think you're going a little overboard?" she asked after a long moment.

"Not really. When I think back through some of the secretaries I've endured in the past, hiring a nanny to keep a good one like you is nothing more than smart business sense."

Actually, there was nothing businesslike going through Conall's mind at the moment, yet he was playing it that way. Otherwise, he knew Vanessa would balk like a stubborn mule at his suggestion.

"Things have happened so quickly I've not yet had time to think of day care for the babies. There might be someone in Hondo to care for the twins while I'm at work," she said a bit tentatively. "Or Lincoln."

He smiled to himself. "Vanessa, we both know you'd be lucky to find a babysitter in either community. And making such a long drive every morning and evening with the babies wouldn't be practical."

She absently pushed at the egg on her plate. "Sometimes a person has to do things that are…well, not the most convenient."

"Why would you need to do that when I can hire someone to watch the babies right in your home? You wouldn't have to disturb them or drag them in and out in the weather. As far as I can see, it's the perfect solution."

She nodded briefly and he could see a range of emotions sweeping across her face. She clearly wanted to resist his help and Conall couldn't understand why. If he'd ever been harsh or cold with the woman, he didn't recall it. And though they'd never visited about things out of the office, he'd never treated her with indifference. He could understand, up to a point, her wanting to be independent. But now wasn't the time for her to worry about showing off her self-reliance. She had more than her own welfare to consider now. Maybe the only way she could think of him was as her boss, instead of a friend offering help. The idea bothered him greatly, although he couldn't figure why it should. He'd stopped caring what women thought of him a long time ago.

She let out a deep breath, then lifted her coffee cup from its saucer. "I'll be honest, Conall. I've been trying to budget in my head and the cost of child care is going to take a big hunk out of my salary. I'd be crazy to turn down your offer of a nanny. At least until the babies get older and I can get my feet planted more firmly."

Relief put a smile on his face. "Now you're making sense. I'll start making calls as soon as we finish breakfast."

"There is one condition, though, Conall."

He paused in the act of reaching for a second piece of toast. "Yes?"

Her brown eyes met his and for a split second his breath hung in his throat. He was slipping, damn it. None of this should feel so important to him. Yes, the babies were adorable and yes, Vanessa's kiss had been like sipping from a honeycomb. But Vanessa and the children weren't supposed to be his business or responsibility.

Her answer broke into his uneasy thoughts. "I also want to have a say in who you hire for the job."

In spite of his internal scolding, Conall began to breathe again. "I wouldn't have it any other way," he assured her.

By the time they finished the last bit of business at the lawyer's office, picked up the babies and boarded a plane back to Ruidoso, Vanessa felt as though she'd gone around the world and back again. The excitement of becoming an instant mother had finally caught up to her, along with the fact that she had no idea of how to deal with this new and different Conall.

The cool, aloof boss that she'd worked with for the past two months appeared to be completely gone. On the flight home, he'd been attentive, reassuring and helpful. When Rick had stirred and began to cry, he'd insisted on cradling the tiny boy in his arms and feeding him one of the bottles the nuns had prepared for their flight.

Seeing the big rancher handle the baby with such gentleness had overwhelmed her somewhat. He was such a man's man and she'd never seen him display much affection toward anyone or anything, except his grandmother Kate and the baby colts and fillies that were born every spring on the Diamond D.

She'd often wondered if his hard demeanor was the thing that had sent his ex-wife, Nancy, running to other pastures. But seeing him interact with her new son had given Vanessa a glimpse of a Conall that she'd never seen or knew existed. There was a soft side to him. So there must have been another, more complicated reason for his divorce.

For weeks now, Vanessa had told herself she didn't want to know what had happened to end her boss's marriage. After all, it wasn't her business and she'd had her own heartbreaking divorce to deal with. But now that Conall had kissed her, now that she'd seen for herself that he could be a hot-blooded man with all sorts of feelings, she'd grown even more curious about his marriage and divorce.

Trying to shove aside the personal thoughts about Conall, Vanessa glanced over her shoulder to see the twins sleeping soundly in the two car seats they'd purchased back in Las Vegas for the trip.

"I doubt the twins will feel any jet lag," Conall commented as he skillfully steered the truck over the mountainous highway toward Tinnie. "They've slept for nearly the entire trip."

She straightened in her seat and as she gazed out the window, she realized she was nearly home. So much had happened since they'd left for Vegas that she felt as though she'd been gone for weeks instead of two days. "That's what newborns mostly do, sleep. Unless they have colic and I'm praying that doesn't happen."

He glanced her way. "You know about babies and colic? I thought you were the youngest of the family."

"I am. But my mother used to reminisce

to me about her babies. She said two of my brothers cried with the colic until they were six months old and she hardly got any sleep during that time."

"I don't suppose she had anyone to help, either. I mean, your dad worked hard and probably needed his rest at night. And she didn't have any older daughters to help out with a crying infant."

"No. My mother didn't have much help with anything. But she was a happy woman." Wistful now, she glanced at him. "I wish Mama could've seen the twins. She would have been so thrilled for me and so proud to have been their grandmother."

To her surprise he reached over and touched her hand with his. "I figure somewhere she does see, Vanessa."

Many of her friends and acquaintances had expressed their sorrow to Vanessa when her mother had died unexpectedly and she'd appreciated all of them. Yet, these simple words from Conall were the most comforting anyone had given her and she was so touched that she was unable to form a reply. The best she could do was cast him a grateful little smile.

He smiled back and she suddenly realized he didn't need or expect her to say anything.

He understood how she felt. The notion not only surprised her, but it also stunned her with uneasy fear. She couldn't allow her feelings for this man to tumble out of control. She had to keep her head intact and her heart safely tucked away in the shadows.

Minutes later Conall parked the truck near the short board fence that cordoned off the small yard from the graveled driveway. After he cut the motor, he said, "Give me the keys and I'll open up before we carry the babies in."

Vanessa dug the house key from her purse and handed it to him. "I'll be unstrapping the twins," she told him.

When he returned, he gathered up Rose from her car seat while Vanessa cradled Rick in the crook of her arm.

Nudging the truck door shut with his broad shoulder, he said, "I'll come back for your luggage and diaper bag later. Right now let's get the babies inside and settled."

Vanessa started to the house with Conall following her onto the tiny porch and past the open door leading into a small living room.

Pausing in the middle of the floor, she glanced around with faint confusion. "Someone has been inside and left the air conditioner on," she said. "I told Maura where the key was but when I last talked to her she didn't mention driving over here."

A sheepish expression stole over his lean face. "I confess. I sent Maura over here to… take care of a few things. I guess she had the forethought to turn on the air conditioner so it would be comfortable when you arrived." He inclined his head toward an arched doorway. "Are the bedrooms through there?"

Vanessa wanted to ask him what sort of things Maura would be doing here. She'd already arranged for a young neighbor boy to feed the goats and the chickens. But seeing he was already changing the subject, she let it pass. She'd be talking to Maura soon enough anyway, she thought.

Nodding in response to his question, she walked past him and he followed her through the doorway and into a tiny hall. As she made a left-hand turn that would lead them to the bedrooms, she said, "My bed is queen-sized so I guess for now, until I get a crib, I'll have to put the twins with me and surround them with pillows."

"Vanessa, why don't you put them in the spare bedroom?"

"Because there's only a narrow twin bed

in there. And everything in there needs to be dusted badly."

"It couldn't be that dusty. And a small bed might work better. Let's look at it."

Vexed that he wanted to argue the matter, she paused to frown at him. "Conall, I told you—"

"Just humor me, Vanessa," he interrupted. "Let me see the room. That's all I'm asking."

How could she deny him such a simple request when he'd just interrupted the past two days of his life to help her? Not to mention absorbing the expense of the trip.

With an indulgent shake of her head, she muttered, "Oh, all right. But I'm beginning to think you'd have been better suited to raise mules than Thoroughbreds, Conall."

He chuckled. "I have a lot of Grandmother Kate in me."

The door to the spare bedroom was slightly ajar and she reached inside to flip on the light before pushing the door wide.

Glancing around at him, she pointed out, "Your grandmother Kate is wonderful. Not stubborn."

"That's what I mean."

The grin on his face made her heart flutter foolishly and she quickly turned her attention away from him to push the bedroom door wide.

"Oh!" The one word was quietly gasped as she stared in complete shock. The dusty drab room that she'd been planning to refurnish one day had been transformed into a fairy-tale nursery. Twisting her head around, she said with stunned accusation, "You knew about this!"

He motioned for her to step inside the room. "Perhaps you should take a look before you decide to chop off my head."

Dazed, she moved slowly into the room while her gaze tried to encompass everything at once. The walls had been painted a soft yellow and bordered with wallpaper of brightly colored stick horses. A classic crib made of dark cherrywood with carved spokes stood in one corner while on the opposite wall a matching chest and dresser framed a window draped with Priscilla curtains printed with the same theme as the wallpaper. Behind them, in another available corner, a full-sized rocking horse made of carved wood, complete with a saddle and a black rag-mop mane and tail waited for little hands and feet to climb on and put him in motion.

"This is…unbelievable," she said in a hushed voice. "It's lovely, Conall. Truly lovely."

"The crib is especially made to connect another one to it later on," he said. "Maura tells me most parents let their twins sleep together until they get a little older. So we thought the one would do for now."

Vanessa stepped over to the bed to see it was made up with smooth, expensive sheets and a yellow-and-white comforter. At the footboard, a mobile with birds and bees dangled temptingly out of reach.

"I think—" She paused as a lump of emotional tears clogged her throat and forced her to swallow. "It's all perfect, Conall."

She pulled back the comforter and placed Rick gently on the mattress. Conall bent forward and laid Rose next to him. Her throat thick, Vanessa watched as he smoothed a finger over the baby girl's red-gold hair, then repeated the same caress on the boy.

Once he straightened away from the babies, he rested his hand against her back and murmured, "I'm glad you think it's perfect, Vanessa. I wanted this little homecoming to be that way for you."

She looked up at him as all sorts of thoughts and questions swirled in her head. "I don't know what to think…or say. The cost, all the work—"

"Don't fret about any of that, Vanessa," he said quickly, cutting her off. "The cost wasn't as much as you think. And the two stable hands that Maura borrowed from the ranch to help her were only too glad to get out of mucking stalls for a couple of days."

Even though Maura and others had worked to prepare the nursery, no one had to tell her that Conall had been the orchestrator of the whole thing and the fact left her totally bewildered. For a man who said he would never have children, Conall was behaving almost like a new father.

What did it mean? Was he doing all this for her? Or the babies? None of it made sense.

Yes, innately he was a good, decent man, she reasoned. And he could afford to be generous. Being his secretary, she personally dealt with the charities he supported, and the people he helped, some of whom he didn't even know. She could almost understand him paying for the trip, the nursery, the nanny. Almost. But the kiss, the touches, the smiles and easy words, those hadn't been acts of charity. Or had they?

"Vanessa? There's a tiny little frown on your forehead. Is something wrong?"

Hoping that was all he could read on her face, she said, "I'm just wondering."

"About what?"

She couldn't answer that, Vanessa decided. If he knew her thoughts had been dwelling on his kiss he'd most likely be amused. And she couldn't stand that. Not from him.

"Nothing. Just forget it," she said dismissively.

He studied her face for a quiet moment, then bent his head and placed a soft kiss on her forehead. "I'm going to go get the rest of your things from the truck," he said gently.

As Vanessa watched him leave the nursery, she realized the twins had done more than made her an instant mother. For now, they'd turned her boss into a different man, one that was very dangerous to her vulnerable heart.

Chapter Five

A week and a half later, Conall stood inside the only barn on the Diamond D that was still the original structure their grandfather, Arthur Donovan, had erected back in the 1960s when the ranch was first established.

The walls of the structure consisted of rough, lapped boards while the wide span of roof was corrugated iron. Down through the years loving attention had allowed the old building to survive the elements and to this day the building was, in his opinion, the prettiest on the ranch.

Conall would be the first person to admit he'd always been attached to the old barn. It held some of his earliest and fondest childhood memories, many of which included his stern grandfather warning him not to climb to the top of the rafter-high hay bales.

"This old building is a tinderbox just waiting for a match or cigarette to come along and ignite it," his brother Liam commented as the two men stood in the middle of the cavernous barn.

For the past few years Liam had been the sole horse trainer for the Diamond D and for the most part Conall allowed him to dictate how the working area of the ranch was laid out and what equipment was needed to keep the horses healthy, happy and in top-notch running and breeding condition. But the old barn was a different matter. It was full of history. It was a point of tradition and Conall was just stubborn enough and old-fashioned enough to insist it remain the same.

"Liam, I've heard this from you a hundred times. You ought to know by now that I have no intention of changing my mind on the subject."

Rolling his eyes with impatience, Liam answered, "Fine. If you don't want to tear the firetrap down, then at least you can renovate and replace the lumber with cinder block."

Conall groaned. "Sorry. I'm not doing that, either. I don't want our ranch to look like the grounds of a penitentiary."

Slapping a pair of leather work gloves against the palm of his hand, Liam muttered, "I don't have to tell you what a fire would do to this place."

The sun had disappeared behind the mountains at least forty-five minutes ago and for the first time in months Conall had left his office earlier than usual with plans to drive to Vanessa's. He didn't want to waste his time going over this worn-out argument with Liam.

"Liam, I might not have my hands on the horses every day like you do, but I do understand their needs and how to care for them. You damn well know that I'm aware of the devastation a fire causes to a horse barn or stables. But—" he used his arm to gesture to the interior of the building "—we're not housing horses in here now. Besides that, we have the most modern and up-to-date fire alarm system installed in every structure on the ranch. Not to mention the fact that we have security guards and stable grooms with the horses around the clock. The horses are safer than our own grandmother is when she's sitting in a rocker on the back porch. So don't give me the fire argument."

Liam let out a disgruntled grunt. "You've got to be the biggest old fogey I know, Conall. What about the argument of updating the barn to make it more usable and efficient? Right now all we have in here are hay and tractor tires!"

"This barn worked for Grandfather and it's still working for us. And right now, it's getting late. Let's get to the house," Conall told him.

With both men agreeing to let the matter drop for now, they stepped out into the rapidly fading light. As they walked to the main house, Liam kept his steps abreast of Conall's.

"I'm going over to the Bar M after dinner," he announced abruptly. "Want to come along?"

Mildly surprised, Conall glanced at him. "The Bar M? The Sanderses giving a party or something?" he asked, then shook his head. "That was a stupid question of me, wasn't it? You don't do parties."

Beneath his cowboy hat, Liam's lips pressed together in a grim line. "Why do you have to be a bastard at times, Conall?"

Conall bit back a sigh. It was true he'd purposely asked the question to dig at his younger brother. But he'd not done it out of meanness as

Liam seemed to think. He'd done it out of care and concern. But trying to explain that to his younger brother would be as easy as making it rain on a cloudless day, he thought dismally.

"I don't know—just goes with my job, I suppose," he quipped.

Liam grunted. "Compared to my job, yours is like a day off. You should be smiling and kicking your heels."

Even though Conall put in long, stressful hours, his job couldn't begin to be compared to Liam's. His younger brother was up at three in the morning in order to be at the stables at four and most nights he didn't fall into bed until long after the rest of the household was sound asleep. When Ruidoso's racing meet wasn't going on, he was shipping horses to tracks in the mid-south and on to the west coast. And their health and racing condition was only a part of his responsibility. He had to make sure each one was strategically entered in a race that would enhance his or her chances of winning.

"I know it," Conall admitted. "That's why you're going to have to give in and replace Clete. Or you're going to end up in the hospital with a heart attack."

Three years ago, Liam's longtime assistant,

Cletis Robinson, had died after a lengthy illness. The death of the seventy-five-year-old man had shaken the whole ranch and especially the Donovan family, who'd valued Clete's friendship for more than thirty years. Liam grunted again. "According to Bridget I don't have a heart."

"She doesn't believe I have one, either," Conall half joked. "I guess our little sister thinks we should be like those namby-pamby guys she went to med school with."

"Bridget is too soft for her own good," Liam muttered.

"So why are you going over to the Bar M this evening?" Conall asked as they approached a side entrance to the main ranch house.

"Chloe has a two-year-old gelding she's thinking about selling. I think he might be good enough to earn some money."

Pausing with surprise, Conall looked at him. "There has to be a catch. Chloe would never sell a good runner."

"Normally, no. But she was forced to geld this one. And Chloe doesn't like to invest time or money into a horse that can't reproduce."

Conall tried not to wince as he reached to open the door. "Yeah," he said, unable to keep the sarcasm from his voice. "Throwing off-spring is the most important thing."

Close on his heels, Liam cursed. "Hell, Conall—"

"Forget I said that," Conall quickly interrupted. "You do what you think about the gelding. I have plans to see the twins tonight."

The two men entered the house and started down a long hallway that would take them to the central part of the house.

"The twins," Liam repeated blankly. "You mean Vanessa's new twins?"

"What other twins do we know?" Conall countered.

Liam stepped up so that the two of them were walking abreast of each other. "Well, there's the Gibson twins. You know, the ones we dated in high school."

Conall chuckled. "So you haven't forgotten them, either?"

Liam grunted with faint humor. "Forget two blonde tornadoes? They might have been short on intelligence but they were long on entertainment," he said, then glanced at Conall. "So what's the deal with Vanessa's twins? I thought after that trip to Las Vegas you had everything taken care of?"

Vanessa and the twins were settled now and

from what she'd told him over the phone, everything was going fine. So why was he giving in to the urge to tear over to her house, Conall asked himself? Because ever since that evening they'd returned from Vegas he'd been dying to see the babies again. And more than that, he missed Vanessa, missed seeing her at her desk and talking with her, however briefly, throughout the busy day.

"They're fine. I have a gift for the babies that I want to deliver."

Liam studied him in faint dismay. "Making a trip out to Vegas and bringing them home wasn't enough of a gift?"

Apparently Liam didn't know about the new nursery he'd funded for the twins or the fact that he was in the process of hunting for a full-time nanny. And Conall wasn't about to tell him. What went on between him and Vanessa was none of Liam's or anyone else's business, he decided.

"No. I wanted to give them something personal. After all, Vanessa is my secretary. And it's not like she had a baby shower." Seeing they'd reached the staircase that led up to the floor where his bedroom and several others were located, he broke away from his brother's side. As he started the climb, he threw a parting comment over his shoulder. "Good luck with Chloe. You're going to need it if you try to deal with her. She's tough."

"She might be tough, big brother, but she's not dangerous."

Conall glanced behind him to see Liam was still standing at the bottom of the stairs staring thoughtfully up at him.

"What does that mean?" Conall asked.

With a dismissive wave, Liam began to move on down the hallway. "You figure it out," he called back to Conall.

From the Diamond D to Vanessa's place, the highway meandered through pine-covered mountains then opened up to bald hills spotted with scrub pinion, twisted juniper and random tufts of grass, and this evening he took in the landscape with renewed appreciation. It wasn't often that Conall left the ranch for any reason. Unless there was an important conference or horse-racing event for him to attend, there wasn't a need for him to leave the isolated sanctuary of his home. Clients came to him, not the other way around.

Going to Vegas with Vanessa had definitely been out-of-character for him. And this trip tonight was even more so, he admitted to himself. Especially since he'd sworn off women and dating.

So what was happening to him? he wondered as he rounded a bend and the turnoff to Vanessa's house came into view. Had two little babies reminded him that his life wasn't over? Or was he simply waking up after a long dormant spell? Either way, it felt good to be getting out, good to think of seeing the babies, and even better to envision kissing Vanessa again.

Vanessa was at the back part of the house in a small alcove used for a laundry room when she heard a faint knock at the front door. Surprised by the unexpected sound, she used her hip to shove the dryer door closed and hurried through the house. In the past few days she'd had a few old friends and acquaintances stop by to see the babies, but it was getting far too late in the evening for such a neighborly visit.

Before opening the door, she peeked through the lacy curtain covering a window that overlooked the front porch. The moment she spotted Conall standing on the tiny piece of concrete, her heart momentarily stopped. He'd not been here since the evening they'd returned from Las Vegas and a few days had passed since she'd talked to him on the phone. It wasn't like her rigidly scheduled boss to show up unannounced on her doorstep. But then it wasn't like Conall to leave the Diamond D, much less leave it to come here.

Momentarily pressing a hand to her chest, she drew in a bracing breath, then pulled the door wide to greet him. This evening he was dressed in old jeans and a predominately white plaid shirt with pearl snaps. A black Stetson was pulled low over his forehead and she was struck by how much younger and relaxed he looked. This was Conall the horseman—not the businessman—and rough sexuality surrounded him like an invisible cloud.

She released the breath she'd been holding. "Hello, Conall."

A sheepish smile crossed his lean features. "Sorry I didn't call first, Vanessa, but I didn't want you thinking you needed to rush around and tidy things before I got here. Am I interrupting?"

Her insides were suddenly shaking, making her feel worse than foolish. For weeks she'd worked with this man every day. It wasn't like he was a stranger. But actually he was a stranger, she thought. This man on her porch wasn't the same as the tough-as-nails boss who ran a multimillion-dollar horse ranch; he was a man she was just beginning to know and like. Far too much.

"Not at all. Won't you come in?" she asked.

"Thanks," he murmured as he stepped through the door.

As he walked to the middle of the small living room, his male scent trailed after him and as her eyes traveled over his broad shoulders and long muscular legs, Vanessa felt her own knees grow ridiculously weak.

"Please have a seat," she offered, "or would you rather take a look at the babies first? They're in the kitchen. Asleep in their bassinet."

Two days after they'd returned from Las Vegas, a delivery truck had arrived at the door with a double bassinet fashioned just for twins. The card accompanying it had simply read, *I thought you might need this, too.*

She'd immediately called Conall and thanked him for the gift, but now that he was here in the flesh, now that his gaze was on her face, she felt extremely exposed and confused. Why was he really here? For her or the babies?

With a guilty little grin, he pulled off the black Stetson and placed it on a low coffee table in front of the couch. "If you don't mind I'd love to see the babies."

"Sure. I was just about to eat. Have you had dinner?" she asked as she motioned for him to follow her out of the room.

"I didn't take time to eat," he admitted. "Liam had me cornered and then it was too late to join the family at the dining table."

"I'm sure Kate wasn't too pleased about that."

He chuckled. "You've heard about Grandmother's strict rules of being on time for dinner?"

Vanessa smiled fondly. "Years ago, when I visited Maura at the ranch, Kate's rules were the first things I learned about the Donovan household. I remember being very scared to enter the dining room."

"Why? Grandmother always loves having young people around."

Shrugging, she entered the open doorway to the kitchen while Conall followed closely behind her. "I always thought I looked too raggedy to sit at her dining table or that I'd say something stupid or wrong."

He shook his head. "Grandmother has never been a snob. Strict, yes, but not a snob. And she made sure the rest of us weren't, either."

"I know. But I always felt a little out of place in your home, Conall." She laughed softly and gestured to the small room they were standing in. It was neat and clean, but the wooden cabinets were more than fifty years old and the porcelain sink chipped and stained. The ceiling was so low that Conall had to duck in order to keep from hitting his head on the light fixture and though the appliances were still chugging along, they'd seen better days. "This isn't quite the same as the kitchen in the Diamond D."

"No," he admitted. "But it's very homey and inviting. And it's yours. That should make you proud."

His comments made her feel warm and good. "It does," she agreed, then motioned to the bassinet sitting near a double window. "I know the babies can't see much yet, but I put them by the window just in case they can pick up the movement of lights and shadows. But I think they notice music more than anything. Whenever I sing to them they usually fall right to sleep. To end the torture, I guess."

Chuckling, Conall crossed the small room and bent over the sleeping babies. "They've grown," he said just above a whisper. "And their skin doesn't look as ruddy."

"They're losing that just-born look," she told him.

He said, "Before you know it they'll be rolling, then crawling and walking. It seems incredible that they start out so tiny and grow into big people like us."

He gazed at them for several long moments before he finally straightened to his full height. When he turned away from the bassinet Vanessa caught sight of his profile and was immediately struck by the wistful expression on his face.

Were the twins softening him? she wondered. Perhaps changing his stance about not having children? She wanted to think so, although she didn't know why the issue was important to her. Whether Conall ever raised a family or not would depend on the next woman he married. Not her and the twins.

He walked over to where she stood by the cabinet counter. "I don't mean this in a bad way, Vanessa, but you look exhausted. I assume the babies are keeping you up at night?"

Unwittingly, she touched a hand to her bare cheek. Without makeup and her hair pulled into a messy knot at the back of her head, she no doubt looked terrible. She hated having him see her like this, but it was too late to worry about her appearance now.

"Some nights are more broken than others," she admitted. "If the babies would both wake at the same time it would be a big help. But Rick always wakes far before his sister and then about the time I get him fed and asleep and I'm about to crawl back into bed, she starts fussing." She smiled at him. "But I'm not complaining. Having the babies...well, it's like a dream come true."

He reached out and rubbed a hand up and down her arm in what was meant to be a comforting gesture. But for Vanessa, it was like flint striking stone. The friction was igniting a trail of tiny flames along her skin, making it difficult for her to breathe.

"You need help, Vanessa. You can't continue to handle two infants alone. I'm sorry it's taken so long for me to find a nanny, but things have been hectic in the office since you've been away."

She sighed. "I'm sorry I've gotten everything out of whack. I did call Fiona and thank her for filling in for me at the office. I hope the job isn't wearing her out."

Conall chuckled. "Wearing Mom out? Not

hardly. She thinks she's still in her twenties instead of entering her sixties."

"She had six children and I'm letting two wear me down," Vanessa said with a grimace. "That makes me feel like a wimp."

"She didn't have two at once. That would wear anyone out. But today I think I might have found a nanny and if things go as planned she'll be over tomorrow or the next day for your approval."

Her interest sparked, Vanessa asked, "Do I know this woman?"

"I doubt it. Her name is Hannah Manning and she's a retired nurse that Maura used to work with at Sierra General."

"Oh. Well, if she's a nurse, she ought to be qualified for the job. I'll look forward to meeting her."

His hand was still on her arm, sending sizzling little signals to her brain, and she could only hope he couldn't guess how much she wanted to touch him, kiss him again. In spite of her days and nights being consumed with caring for the twins, she'd not been able to quit thinking about the man.

"I've stewed a pot of *carne guisada* for dinner," she said, her gaze awkwardly avoiding his. "Would you like to join me?"

"I'd love to," he murmured, "but I'd like to do something else first."

She was wondering what *something else* could possibly be when his forefinger slid beneath her chin and lifted her face up to his. Their gazes clashed and Vanessa's heart began to thud so hard she could scarcely breathe.

"Conall, this…is…not good," she finally managed to whisper.

His mouth twisted to a sexy slant. "How do you know that? We haven't done it yet."

She groaned with misgivings but the sound didn't deter him. Instead, both his hands came up to frame the sides of her face. The tender intimacy shot her resistance to tiny pieces and as his head lowered toward hers, she closed her eyes and leaned into him.

This time the meeting of their mouths was not the fragile exploration they'd exchanged in Las Vegas. No, this time it was all-out hunger, and what little breath Vanessa had beforehand was instantly swept away by the crush of his hard lips.

Instinctively her hands grabbed for support and landed smack in the middle of his chest. She gripped folds of his cotton shirt as the heat of his body infused hers with heady warmth and his hands began a lazy expedition against her shoulders.

Certain she was going to dissolve in a helpless puddle if the kiss went any further, Vanessa frantically tore herself away and turned her back to him.

She was fiercely trying to fill her lungs with oxygen, when his lips pressed against her ear and she closed her eyes as he began to whisper, "I'm not going to apologize for that, Vanessa. It felt too right."

She couldn't argue that point. Until now, until Conall's lips had touched hers, no man's kiss had ever spun her away to such a fairy-tale world. And that was the problem, she thought desperately. Conall was a prince and he wasn't looking to make her his princess.

She swallowed hard. "I don't expect you to apologize," she said in a faint voice. "I'm just—" Stiffening her resolve, she turned back to him. "I don't know what's going through your mind, Conall. But I think you should understand that I'm not a woman who plays around."

For a fraction of a second, he looked astounded and then a grimace tightened his features. "Do you think I'm a man who plays around?"

Her eyes searched his. "I've never thought so. But you're starting to make me wonder."

He let out a mocking snort. "I haven't touched another woman in a long, long time. Does that sound like a man that's on the prowl?"

It sounded like a man who was still in love with his ex-wife, or one that had been wounded so badly he'd turned away from love altogether. Either way, Vanessa thought, the notion was a bleak one.

Sighing heavily, she stepped around him and crossed over to a small gas range. Giving one of the knobs a savage twist, she ignited a flame beneath a blue granite pot.

After a moment, she answered his question. "No. It sounds to me like a man that's confused."

"Confused, hell," he muttered.

She glanced over her shoulder to see him striding toward her and before she could stop it, desire washed through her like a hot wave, knocking down her defenses before she could even get them erected.

"Well, if you're not mixed up, I am," she admitted.

He stopped within a few inches of her and though he didn't touch her, Vanessa could almost feel his hands, his gaze, roaming her face, her body.

"Explain that, would you?"

A war exploded inside her and she was trying to decide if she wanted to throw herself in his arms or scurry out of the room, when he shifted closer.

She tried to swallow but her throat was so dry she nearly choked in the process. Finally, she managed to say, "I don't understand any of this, Conall."

He was looking at her with that same stony expression she'd seen on him in the office when things weren't going his way.

"It would help if I knew what *this* was," he stated.

The fact that he was deliberately being ignorant made her clench her jaw tight and suddenly all the doubts and emotions that had been swirling around in her for the past two weeks boiled to the surface. "You know what I'm talking about, Conall!" she burst out. "I've worked for you every day for more than two months and you hardly took a moment to look at me, much less touch me. Now all of a sudden you behave as though I'm irresistible. It's—it's ridiculous! That's what it is."

Behind her the stewed beef began to boil

rapidly and the sound matched the blood pounding in her ears. Twisting around to the stove, she automatically lowered the flame as she sucked in a deep breath and tried to calm herself. But the effort failed completely as soon as his hands settled upon her shoulders.

"Vanessa, I don't understand why you're so worked up over a kiss," he murmured. "I'm not asking you to jump into bed with me."

The mere idea of making intimate love to this man was enough to make her face flame and her body burn. And she suddenly felt terribly, terribly embarrassed. Maybe she was acting foolish and naive. Maybe she was making a mountain out of a molehill.

Forcing herself to turn and face him, she said, "I'm sorry, Conall, but this change in our relationship has caught me off guard. I wasn't expecting any of this and—"

"Do you think I was? Hell, Vanessa, like I said before I've not even looked in a woman's direction in years. And even after you came to work for me I wasn't thinking of you in this way, but..."

She waited for him to finish, but he appeared to be lost for words.

"But what, Conall? I receive word about the

babies and suddenly you're looking at me as though you've never seen me before."

"That's true," he admitted.

Incredulous, Vanessa stared at him. "It is?"

Clearly frustrated, he swiped a hand through his dark brown hair. "I can't give you a solid reason for my behavior, Vanessa, except that the day you fainted in the office I began to see you as a woman."

Grimacing, she peered around him to the opposite side of the room. Thankfully, the twins were still sleeping soundly in their bassinet.

"And what was I before?" she asked dryly, "A robot that answered the phone and dealt with your correspondence?"

He groaned. "I'm trying to explain."

"You're not doing a very good job of it," she pointed out.

His hands slipped from her shoulders and slid down her arms until they reached her hands. Then, like a pair of flesh-and-bone handcuffs, his fingers clamped around her wrists.

"You're not making the task any easier, either," he countered.

Nervously moistening her lips, she focused her gaze to the middle button on his shirt. "I suppose I'm not," she admitted. "But try to see things from my angle, Conall. Suddenly you're making the twins a nursery, buying them gifts and—and handling me as though…you want to! What am I suppose to think? Are you playing up to me just so you can be around the twins?"

"That's damned stupid!"

Surprised by sharpness in his voice, her gaze flew up to his face.

"I care about the twins," he went on. "But I'm pretty sure you'd let me visit them whether I kissed you or not."

Desperate for answers, she spluttered at him, "So why are you kissing me? Because your libido has woken up and I'm handy?"

His nostrils flared as his fingers tightened on her wrists. "Vanessa, none of this is hard to understand. I'm simply being a man. A man that has found himself attracted to a woman. A kiss is…well, I'm trying to tell you that I think we should get to know each other better. On a more personal level."

She groaned with disbelief. "That wasn't a get-to-know-you kiss, Conall. That was more like an I-missed-you-like-hell kiss."

To her amazement, a tempting little grin spread across his lips. "Finally, you're getting something right," he murmured, his eyes settling softly on her face. "I have missed you like hell."

His admission sent a foolish thrill rushing through her, spinning her heartbeat to a rapid thud.

"That's very hard to believe," she said, in a breathless whisper.

"Then maybe I'd better give you another demonstration. Just to prove my point."

Making his intentions clear, his head bent toward hers and though Vanessa told herself she'd be smart to make a quick escape, she couldn't make a move. Instead, she stood transfixed and waited for his lips to capture hers.

Chapter Six

Just a few more moments, Vanessa promised herself, and then she'd gather the strength to step away from the heated search of Conall's lips. She'd get her breath back, along with her senses, and then she'd remind herself why being in his arms was as dangerous as sidling up to a sizzling stick of dynamite.

But so far the minutes continued to tick away and she'd not taken that first move to end their kiss. Instead, she couldn't stop her lips from parting beneath his, her arms from sliding around his waist.

She was leaning into him, her whole body buzzing with the anticipation of getting even closer to his hard body, when she caught the sound of Rick's faint whimpers.

The pressure of Conall's lips eased just a fraction, telling her that he must have picked up on the baby's subtle call. Even so, he didn't bother to end the kiss until the tiny boy let loose with an all-out cry.

Lifting his head, he drew in a ragged breath and glanced over his shoulder toward the bassinet. "That child needs to learn better timing," he said with humor, then glancing back to Vanessa, he added, "Sounds like duty calls."

Struggling to regain her composure, she said in a husky voice, "It's Rick. I can tell by his cry. He's probably thinking it's time for his supper, too."

After switching off the fire beneath the *carne guisada*, she walked over to the bassinet. Conall followed close on her heels.

"Can I help?" he asked.

She lifted the fussing Rick from the bed. "It would be a big help if you could hold him while I heat a bottle."

Conall eagerly held out his arms. "I'd be glad to hold him, just don't expect me to make him stop crying," he warned. "I wouldn't know how."

She carefully placed the baby in the crook

of Conall's strong arm. "Just rock him a little," she suggested. "And don't worry if he keeps on crying. He's not hurting, just exercising his opinion."

Chuckling, he looked down at the fussy baby. "Oh, well, we men have to do that from time to time."

Pausing for just a moment, Vanessa couldn't help but take in the sight of Conall with tiny Rick cradled against his broad chest. The man looked like a born father, she thought, certainly not a guy that had sworn off having children.

Shaking away that disturbing notion, Vanessa hurried to the refrigerator to fetch the bottle. She was about to place it in the microwave, when Rose decided to let loose with a wail.

"I think you'd better make it two bottles," Conall said, raising his voice above the crying.

"So I hear."

Vanessa collected another bottle from the refrigerator and quickly heated them to a wrist-warm temperature. By the time she handed Conall one of the bottles and went to gather Rose from the bassinet, the girl was howling at the top of her lungs.

"I think you'll find it easier to feed him if you're sitting down," Vanessa told Conall, then she picked up Rose and crooned soothingly to the baby while carrying her over to the dining table.

After taking a seat, Vanessa propped the baby in the crook of her arm and offered her the bottle. Rose latched on to the nipple and began to nurse hungrily.

On the opposite side of the table Conall was trying to emulate Vanessa's movements. "I've never fed a baby before," he admitted. "I'm not sure I'm doing any of this right."

From what Vanessa could see the Donovan family had been having babies left and right with Maura's two boys and Brady's little girl. She found it difficult to believe that Conall hadn't given at least one of them a bottle. Especially Brady's daughter, since the two brothers lived together in the main ranch house. Sure, he was a busy man, she reasoned, but not that busy. Perhaps the babies had all been breast-fed. That might account for his lack of experience, she thought.

"There's nothing to it," she assured him. "Just keep his head supported and the bottle tilted upward so he won't suck air. He'll do the rest."

He shifted Rick to a comfortable position and offered him the bottle. Once the baby was nursing quietly, Conall looked over at Vanessa and smiled. "Hey, that's quite a silencer. Does a bottle always do the trick?"

Vanessa chuckled. "Unfortunately, no. Sometimes they cry when they aren't hungry and I have to try to figure out what's wrong and what they're trying to tell me."

He nodded. "Like a horse. They can't talk with words, but they have other ways of communicating."

It wasn't a surprise to Vanessa to hear Conall use equine terminology. Even though he didn't spend his days down at the barns as Liam did, he was equally as knowledgeable about the animals. In fact, the first time she'd seen Conall up close was when she'd visited the Diamond D and she and Maura had walked down to the training area where Conall had been breezing a huge black Thoroughbred around an oval dirt track. At the time he'd been a lean teenager, not the muscular man he was now. Yet she'd remembered being impressed by his strength and the easy way he'd handled the spirited stallion.

Needless to say, from that moment on he'd been her dark, secret prince and she'd dreamed of how incredible it would be to be the object of his affection. But then he'd graduated from high school and left for college. Vanessa had put away her crush for the rich Donovan boy and focused on the reality of her future, one that included leaving Lincoln County, New Mexico, and her adolescent dreams behind.

"Vanessa, you've gone far way. What are you thinking?"

Unaware that she'd gotten so lost in her thoughts, her face warmed with a blush as she glanced over at him. "Actually, I was thinking back to the first time I saw you," she admitted.

The lift of his dark brows said she'd surprised him.

"Really? You remember that?"

Clearly his memory bank didn't include the first time he'd seen her, but then she hardly expected him to recall such a thing. He'd been older and had moved in much higher social circles than she. He'd always been associated with the brightest and prettiest girls on the high school campus. He would have never bothered to give someone like her a second glance.

"I do. You were on the track, exercising one of your father's horses."

He chuckled with fond remembrance. "Hmm. That must have been when I was thirty pounds lighter."

"You were about seventeen."

With a shake of his head, he murmured, "So long ago."

"I had a huge crush on you."

The moment the words passed her lips, Vanessa expected amusement to appear on his face, or even a laugh to rumble out of him. Instead, he studied her thoughtfully for a long, long spell and Vanessa got the impression he was thinking back to those carefree days before either of them had met their respective spouses.

"I didn't know," he said finally.

She felt the blush on her face sting her cheeks even hotter. To escape his searching gaze, she bent her head over Rose's sweet little face.

"No," she murmured, as she absently adjusted the receiving blanket around the baby's shoulders. "I would have died with embarrassment if you'd found out. In fact, I never told anyone about my feelings for you. Not even my mother."

"And why was that?" he quietly asked.

That pulled her attention back to him and she smiled wanly. "Mama was a realist. She would have given me a long lecture about crying for the moon."

His brows formed a line of disapproval. "You make it sound like I was some sort of unattainable prize, Vanessa."

"To me you were."

His head swung back and forth. "I was just a young man, like millions of others in the world."

Not to her. Not then. Not now, Vanessa thought. With a shake of her head, she gave him a patient smile. "Conall, look around. You didn't pick your girlfriends from this sort of background. Nor would you now."

Rolling his eyes toward the ceiling, he mouthed a curse under his breath. "I don't have girlfriends now. I've already told you that." He lowered his gaze back to her face. "Unless I count you as one."

Her heart gave a jerk. "Is that what I am to you?"

A slow grin tilted the corners of his lips. "I think that's a subject we need to discuss, don't you?"

Was he serious? No. He couldn't be. But, oh, his kiss had felt very, very serious. And that scared her. She wasn't emotionally capable of dealing with a man like him. "No. That's out of the question."

"Why?"

She couldn't stop the tiny groan from sounding in her throat. "I could give you a whole list of reasons. The main one being we have to work with each other."

"So? I can't see that posing a problem. Neither of us are married or committed to someone else."

"It would make things awkward," she said flatly. "Impossible, in fact."

Seeing that Rose had quit nursing and fallen asleep, Vanessa placed the near empty bottle on the table. Rising to her feet, she carefully positioned the baby against her shoulder and gently patted her back. As soon as she heard a loud burp, she carried the sleeping girl back to the bassinet.

"I think he's finished eating, too," Conall told her. "But he's not asleep. His eyes are wide open."

"He probably won't cry now if you put him back by his sister," she suggested as she crossed the room to pull dishes from the cabinet. "But you need to burp him first."

"I might need a little help with that."

Leaving the task of the dishes behind, she walked back over to where he sat holding the baby. "Place him against your shoulder or across your lap," she instructed.

Slowly, he adjusted the boy so that he was reclined against his shoulder.

"Now what?"

"Pat him gently on the back."

He frowned at her. "I don't know what you consider gentle."

She rolled her eyes. "Well, I don't mean pat him like you would a horse's neck!" Deciding it would be easier to show him, she picked up Conall's hand and placed a few measured pats against Rick's back.

"Okay, I get—"

Before he could complete the rest of his sentence, Rick made a belching noise, which was immediately followed by Conall's yelp.

Vanessa didn't have to ask what had happened. She could see a thick stream of milk oozing from Rick's mouth and rolling down Conall's back.

"Uggh! Is that what I think it is?" he asked, twisting his head around in order to get a glimpse of his soggy shoulder.

"Sorry," she said, and before she could stop herself she began to laugh.

He flashed a droll look at her. "I didn't know being vomited on was so funny."

"It isn't. But—" She was laughing so hard she couldn't finish, but instead of him getting angry, he began to grin.

He said, "I didn't know you could laugh like that."

She calmed herself enough to say, "I didn't know you could look so...dumbfounded, either."

He thrust the baby at her. "Here, you'd better take the little volcano before he erupts again."

Still chuckling, Vanessa lifted Rick from his arms. While she cleaned the baby's face, Conall snatched up several paper towels and attempted to wipe the burp from the back of his shirt.

"I'll help you do that," Vanessa told him. "Just let me get Rick settled back in the bassinet."

Once she had both babies nestled together in their bed, she walked over to where Conall stood at the kitchen sink.

"You smell like formula," she said.

"No kidding."

She motioned for him to turn his back to her. When he did, she groaned with dismay.

"Oh, Conall, this is beyond wiping. You're going to have to take off your shirt and let me wash it for you."

"That's too much trouble. Surely the mess will dry."

"Eventually," she agreed. "But I don't think

either of us will enjoy eating our supper with that smell at the dining table." She motioned with her hand for the shirt. "Give it to me. I have other things to wash anyway. And if you're worried about sitting around half-naked, I'll find you one of Dad's old shirts."

"All right, all right," he mumbled, then quickly began to strip out of the garment.

Vanessa tried not to stare as the fabric parted from his chest and slipped off his shoulders. Still, it was impossible to keep her gaze totally averted from his muscled chest, the dark patch of hair between his nipples and the hard abs disappearing into the waistband of his jeans.

"I'll put it right in the machine," she said in a rush, then hurried out of the room before she made a complete idiot out of herself.

A man's anatomy was nothing new to her, she reminded herself as she tossed Conall's shirt into the washing machine and followed it with a few more garments. She'd been married for five years and Jeff had been a physically attractive man. Yet looking at him without his shirt hadn't left her breathless or tongue-tied, the way looking at Conall had a moment ago.

Trying not to reason that one out, Vanessa went to a closet where she'd stored some of her father's clothing in hopes that one day he'd get well enough to come home and wear them again. Now she pulled out a dark blue plaid shirt and hurried back to the kitchen.

When she stepped through the doorway, she spotted Conall sitting at the table and she swallowed hard as she walked over and handed him the shirt. "Here's something to wear while you're waiting. It might be a little big," she warned. "Dad was pretty fleshy before he had the stroke."

"Thanks, I'm sure it'll be fine."

Rising to his feet, he plunged his arms into the sleeves of the cotton shirt. To her surprise the shirt wasn't all that big, proof that her eyes hadn't deceived her when they had taken in the sight of his broad shoulders and thick chest.

"So now that the babies are settled and you don't smell like a half-soured milk factory, are you ready to eat?" she asked.

"Sure. Can I help with anything?" he asked as he followed her over to the cabinets.

"Have you honestly ever done anything in the kitchen? Besides eat?"

"Well, I—" He thought for a moment, then gave her a sly grin. "I put the teakettle on to boil whenever I need steam to reshape my hat."

She let out a good-natured groan. "Oh. So

you know how to boil water. That's something."

He chuckled. "Maybe you could teach me a few things. Just in case the Diamond D kitchen staff ever go on strike."

His comment reminded Vanessa of the privileged life he led, the fortune he'd been born into.

"I wouldn't worry about it," she replied. "You can always hire someone else to do the job for you."

As she began to pull down plates again, he came to stand close behind her.

"Do you resent that fact, Vanessa? That I… and my family have money? I never thought so. But—" One hand came to rest against the back of her shoulder. "We've never talked about personal things before."

She gripped the edges of the plates as unbidden desire rushed through her.

"We were always too busy to make personal chitchat." She glanced over her shoulder. "But as far as you being wealthy, I don't resent that. You work harder than anybody I know."

"Not Liam," he corrected.

With the plates pressed against her chest, she turned to face him. "No. Maybe not Liam," she agreed. "But you're just as dedicated."

He gently brushed the back of his knuckles against her cheek and Vanessa wanted to slip into his arms.

"I'm glad you think I earn what I have. And I'll tell you something else, Vanessa, I like spending it on you—and the babies. I like making things better for you. It makes all the work I do mean more to me."

Every cell inside her began to tremble. "That's not the way it should be, Conall. We're—the babies and I...well, you should be doing all of that for a family of your own. Not us."

Slowly, he eased the plates from her tight grip. "Yeah," he said, his quiet voice full of cynicism. "That might be good advice, Vanessa. But I don't happen to have a family of my own."

He carried the plates over to the table and all of a sudden she was struck by the fact that in spite of Conall's wealth, in spite of his long list of valuable assets, he didn't have what she had. He didn't have two tiny babies who needed and cried for his touch or quieted at the soothing sound of his voice. He didn't have anyone to call him Daddy. And from what he'd told Vanessa, he never would.

Hot moisture stung the back of her eyes and

as she turned to fish silverware from a small drawer, she wondered whether the unexpected tears were for Conall or herself.

Chapter Seven

Nearly two weeks later, Conall was sitting at his desk, watching dusk settle across the ranch yard when Fiona stepped into the room and announced she was quitting for the day.

"Your father and grandmother will be ready to eat in thirty minutes. Will you be there?" his mother asked.

"Uh...no." Struggling to focus his thoughts back to the moment, he glanced over to Fiona. The woman had been working nonstop all day at Vanessa's desk, yet she looked nearly as fresh as she had when she'd started at eight this morning. Her graceful femininity was a guise, he couldn't help thinking. She was actually a lioness, always fierce and never tiring. "I'm afraid not. I still have a few calls to make before I leave the office."

She grimaced. "Have you talked to Liam?"

"No. Why?"

"He wanted to speak with you about Blue Heaven—the two-year-old. Something about paying her futurity fees."

Leaning back in his chair, he looked at her with puzzlement. "Why would Liam want to talk to me about the filly? Liam is the trainer, he enters any horse he wants into whatever race he wants. He certainly doesn't ask my opinion on the matter."

Frowning with impatience, she stepped farther into the office until she was standing at the end of his desk. Conall felt as if time had traveled back to when he was ten years old and he'd slipped off to the horse barn instead of doing his homework.

"Does it ever cross your mind that your brother needs your support? That he might want your advice on these matters?"

His gaze dropping away from his mother, he picked up a pen and began to tap it absently against the ink blotter. He wasn't in the mood for one of Fiona's family lectures. He was missing Vanessa like hell and though a

nanny for the twins had been hired more than
a week ago, she'd not yet returned to work.
And damn it, he wasn't going to push her, even
though he wanted to. "Not really."

To his surprise Fiona muttered a curse under
her breath. It was rare that he ever heard his
mother utter a foul word and he couldn't imagine this trivial matter pulling one from her
mouth.

"Not really," she mimicked with sarcasm. "I
should have known that would be your answer.
I doubt you actually think about your brother
for more than five minutes out of the day!"

Startled by her unexpected outburst, he
jerked his head up to stare at her. "What in
the world are you talking about, Mom? Is this
'feel sorry for Liam' day or something?"

"Don't get smart with me, Conall. This is as
much about you as it is about Liam working
himself to death."

Conall tossed down the pen. "Maybe you
haven't noticed, but I'm not exactly taking a
vacation here," he muttered, then immediately
shook his head. "Sorry, Mom. I...shouldn't
have said that."

"No. You shouldn't have."

Sighing with exasperation, he swiveled his
chair so that he was facing her head-on. "Liam

is working too hard. But what can I do about it? I've been after him to hire an assistant. But he doesn't think anyone could measure up to Clete. Until he decides that he's not going to find another Clete and hires someone to help him, there's not much I can do."

Fiona sighed. "That's true. But I wish…well, that you would take time for him and he would take time for you. You're both so damned obsessed with work that—" Pausing, she shook her head with regret. "Forget it, Conall. I can't change either of you and it's wrong of me to try. I just want you to be happy. But Liam goes around pretending everything is just dandy when it's anything but. And you—sometimes I think you've simply given up. A son of mine," she added with disgust, "I never thought I'd see it."

It wasn't like Fiona to be so critical. Even when she was angry with her children, she managed to display it in a loving way. But something seemed to have stirred her up. As for him giving up, it was no secret that his parents wanted him to get back into the dating scene and find himself a wife. To the Donovans, a person had nothing unless they had a family. And they both had the Pollyanna idea that if he found the right woman, she would understand and accept his sterile condition. Maybe there were a few out there, he thought dully. But would one of them be a woman he could love?

Hell. What kind of question is that, Conall? You don't believe in love anymore. Not after Nancy. Why can't you settle for someone to simply cozy up to and grow old with? Your heart doesn't have to be involved.

His jaw tight, he said firmly, "I'm sorry you've had to work so hard these last few weeks, Mom. I thought Vanessa would have been back by now. But—"

She looked at him sharply. "I can manage this office with one hand tied behind my back. That's not—" She waved a dismissive hand at him and started out the door. "I've got to get back to the house for dinner. And you won't be seeing me at Vanessa's desk in the morning. She called a few minutes ago to say she'd be returning tomorrow."

His boots hit the floor with a thump. "Vanessa called? Why didn't she speak to me?"

"You were on the phone with the fencing company. She didn't want to disturb you."

Or maybe she'd simply wanted to avoid talking to him, Conall thought as his mother slipped out the door. But that was a stupid notion. She was coming back to work tomorrow. She'd be spending her days with him. But it wasn't exactly the days that Conall had been thinking about before his mother had walked in and abruptly interrupted his musings.

With a heavy sigh, he rose from the deep leather chair and walked over to a large framed window overlooking part of the stables. Resting his shoulder against the window seal, he gazed out at the lengthening shadows. Ranch hands were busy with the evening chores and no doubt Liam was in one of the barns, making sure his latest runners were pampered and happy.

Liam goes around pretending everything is just dandy when it's anything but. And you— sometimes I think you've simply given up.

Fiona's words were still rattling around in his head and though Conall tried to tell himself they were simply a mother expressing dissatisfaction with her sons, he had to admit she was, at least, partially right. He couldn't speak for Liam, but as for himself, he supposed he had given up on some aspects of his life.

Didn't his mother realize it was easier for him to focus on his work instead of the mess he'd made of his personal life? The mess he would make if he tried to marry again?

You should be doing all of that for a family of your own. Not us.

Close on the heels of his mother's words, Vanessa traipsed through his mind, reminding him just how much she and the twins had changed his life, had reopened the old dreams and wishes that he'd started out with as a young man.

Although he'd talked with Vanessa on the phone about hiring the nanny, he'd not seen her since the night Rick had burped all over him. Every night since then, he'd wanted to go back to her house. He'd wanted to sit across from her at the little table, eat warm tortillas, talk about mundane things and simply watch her beautiful face. Over and over he'd thought about the way she'd felt in his arms when he'd kissed her and the way she'd looked afterward. For the first time in a long time he'd wanted to make love to a woman. And though he'd told himself he'd been too busy to make the trip over to Tinnie to see her, a part of him knew he'd been hiding these past few days, afraid to admit to himself or to her that she and the babies were the family he'd wanted for so long.

Three days later, Vanessa was relieved that Friday had finally arrived. If she didn't get out of the office and away from Conall soon, she was either going to break into pieces or throw herself into his arms and beg the man to make love to her. Neither option was suitable for a secretary who'd always considered herself a professional. And she was beginning to wonder if the job she'd once loved was now going to have to come to an end.

Drawing in a bracing breath, she rapped her knuckles on the door separating their offices. The moment she heard him calling for her to enter, she stepped into his domain and shut the door behind her.

"I have the contract for the trucking company ready for you to sign," she said as she approached his desk. "I've also alerted Red Bluff that a new trucking company will be in place at the mine by the middle of next month."

"Good. I'm glad to get that settled." He glanced up as she leaned forward to place the papers in front of him. "Did Red Bluff seem to have any problem with the idea of new haulers?"

It was after five in the evening and though he'd started out the day in a crisply starched shirt and matching tie, the tie was now loosened and the top two buttons of his shirt were undone while the sleeves were rolled back on his forearms. His nearly black hair was rumpled and she knew if she were to rub her cheek against his, she'd feel the faint rasp of his beard.

"Not at all," she said as she straightened to her full height and tried to bring her thoughts to the business at hand.

"Good. I only wish raising racehorses was as easy as digging gold from a mountainside." He picked up a pen and scratched his name on the appropriate lines. Once he was finished, he handed the document back to her and smiled. "But my grandfather used to say that nothing was worthwhile, unless it was earned. Gold mines eventually peter out. Horses will always be."

"Yes, well, I'll get this in the outgoing mail before I leave this evening," she told him, then quickly turned to start out of the room.

She'd taken two steps when his hand closed around her upper arm and with a mental groan, she turned to face him.

"Was there something else?" she asked.

Grimacing at her businesslike tone, he muttered, "Hell, yes, there's plenty more! I want to know why you've been acting as though I have a contagious disease. Ever since you've started back to work, you've been tiptoeing around me like I'm some sort of hulking monster."

Shaking her head, she looked away from him and swallowed hard. "I'm sorry if it appears that way, Conall. But I'm just trying to keep things in order."

"What does that mean?"

"It means—" Her gaze slipped to her arm, where his fingers were pressed like dark brown bands around her flesh. "I'm trying to keep our relationship professional here in the office."

He stepped closer and her heart began to knock against her ribs. "What if I don't want it to be professional?" he asked softly.

She cleared her throat, but it didn't clear away the huskiness in her voice when she spoke. "Like I told you before, Conall, we can't—"

Before she could get the rest of her words out, he jerked her forward and into his arms. The instant his lips covered hers, Vanessa understood why she'd been fighting so hard to keep this very thing from happening.

Tasting his kiss again, having his arms holding her close against his hard body, felt incredibly delicious and impossible to resist. She couldn't hide or ignore the desire rushing through her, urging her to open her mouth to his and slip her arms up and around his neck.

All at once the kiss heated, deepened and surrounded her senses in a hot fog. The room receded to a dim whirl around her head. She heard his groan and then his hands were sliding down her back, splaying against her buttocks and dragging her hips toward his.

Crushed in the intimate embrace, Vanessa forgot they were in his office and that anyone could walk in on them. She forgot, that is, until the phone in her office began to ring and stop, then ring again.

Summoning on all the strength she could find, she jerked her mouth from his. "Conall—the phone, I—"

"Forget the phone," he ordered huskily as his mouth descended toward hers for a second time. "The caller can leave a message."

Panicked by just how much she wanted to do his bidding, she burst out, "No!"

Twisting away from his embrace she started to hurry out of the room, but halfway to the door, she realized at some point during their kiss she'd dropped the contract.

Turning back, she groaned when she spotted it lying to one side of his boots. As she walked toward him to retrieve it, he said softly, "That was a quick change of mind."

"I haven't changed my mind." She bent down to retrieve the typed pages that were held together with a heavy paper clip. "I'm retrieving the contract. That's all."

Gripping the document with both hands, she straightened back to her full height and before she could step away his hand came out to catch her by one elbow.

"All right, Vanessa, you can pretend you're indifferent, but I won't believe it," he murmured.

She swallowed as her heartbeat reacted to his nearness. "Conall, I'm not going to deny that I like kissing you. But—"

"Good," he interrupted before she could go on. "Because I plan on us doing a lot more of it."

"No," she repeated. "It won't take us anywhere. Except to bed!"

A corner of his mouth curled upward. "For once we agree on something."

She stared at him as her mind spun with questions and images that left her face burning with red heat. "Well, you might as well go over to your desk and write this down on your calendar, Conall—it ain't gonna happen!"

He laughed in a totally confident way, but instead of the sound irking her, it sent a scare all the way down to her feet. To make love to Conall would be the end of her. He'd have her eating out of his hand, waiting and begging for any crumbs of affection he might throw her way.

"You look very pretty when you use bad grammar. Did you know that?"

She muttered a helpless curse and then the phone began to ring again. "The one thing I do know is that I have to get back to work and—"

"No. You don't. It's quitting time," he said, his voice quickly slipping back to boss mode. "And right now I want to speak with you about tomorrow night."

She arched her brows at him. "Tomorrow night? Are you having a special meeting or something and I need to attend to take notes?"

He shook his head. "Not even close. Sunday is Grandmother Kate's birthday and the family is throwing her a party. Not anything as huge as we did for her eightieth. But since this is her eighty-fifth we thought she deserved more than just a cake and a few gifts from her family."

"What does this have to do with me? You'd like for me to pick up a gift or flowers for you to give to her?"

He frowned. "Not hardly. I know how to buy gifts for women. Even one as hard to please as Kate." His hand departed her elbow and began a hot glide up her bare arm and onto her shoulder. "I'd like for you to attend the party with me. Will Hannah be available to watch after the twins?"

He was inviting her to his family home? As his companion? She couldn't believe it. Sure, as a young teenager she'd been inside the small mansion many times. But that had been totally different. She'd been there as Maura's friend, not as a so-called date for the eldest Donovan son.

"So far I can't get Hannah to take any time off, so she will be available. But I'm not keen on the idea of being away from the babies for that long. I know that probably sounds silly to you, but just being apart from them while I'm here at the office has been hard for me to deal with these past three days."

He smiled with understanding. "It's not silly. You're a new mother. But it's not a problem, either. You can bring the twins to the party with you."

Her jaw dropped. "To the party? Conall, they're only a few weeks old."

"I'm well aware of how old they are. Everyone will love seeing them. In fact, the whole family has been asking about them."

How could she turn down the invitation now, she wondered, without appearing to be indifferent to his family? She couldn't. "If you think no one will mind," she said hesitantly.

"Grandmother will love seeing the babies. Bring Hannah, the nanny, too," he added. "That way you won't be babysitting the whole time. And Hannah is acquainted with Maura and Bridget, so I'm sure she'll enjoy the outing, too."

Another reason why she couldn't refuse, Vanessa thought wryly. Hannah, the nanny that Conall had hired for the twins, was a lovely widow and worked tirelessly to keep the babies healthy and happy. So far she'd not taken a night off for any reason and Vanessa knew the woman needed a break of some sort.

"All right. We'll be there. But I don't understand any of this, Conall. Why invite me? Now? Since I've come to work for you, your family has held several parties for one reason or another. You didn't ask me to attend any of those," she couldn't help pointing out.

"Look, Vanessa, whatever you might think or want, the two of us aren't going back to the impersonal relationship we had before the twins arrived. Things have changed with you and with me. Surely I don't have to spell that out to you."

Things have changed. That was certainly an understatement, she thought. If she wasn't with the man, she was thinking about him. And when she was with him all she could think about was being in his arms. She was in a predicament that was very unhealthy to her state of mind and try as she might, she couldn't seem to do a thing about it.

"I think—" She broke off abruptly as the phone began to ring again.

"You think what?" he prompted.

She shook her head. Now wasn't the time or place to say the things she needed to say to him. Tomorrow night would be soon enough to let him know he was sniffing around the wrong tree. "Nothing. I'll be at the party, Conall. With Rose and Rick. Right now I'm going to get this contract in the mail, then go home."

He looked like he wanted to say more, or maybe it was more kissing he had on his mind. Whatever it was she read on his face, she didn't hang around to let him put his wants into action. She hurried out of the room and purposely shut the door between them.

* * *

Apparently Mother Nature didn't want to disappoint the Donovans. With Kate's party being held in the backyard beneath the pines and the cottonwood trees, the early August weather couldn't have been more perfect. Even the mosquitoes seemed to forget to come out after night had fallen and the colorful party lanterns were glowing festively over the tables of food that had been served more than an hour ago.

Conall had told her the party was going to be small, but to Vanessa it was anything but. People, most of whom she didn't know, filled the yard and the back porch where Kate was presently ensconced in a rattan chair surrounded by family and friends. Music was playing and down by the pool the more active guests were laughing and splashing and swimming in the crystal blue water.

Tilting the long-stemmed glass to her lips, Vanessa drained the last of her punch while wondering how soon she could leave without appearing unsociable. She'd already spoken to Kate and expressed her well wishes. She'd chatted at length with Maura and exchanged a few words with the rest of the Donovans. Except for Conall. So far she'd seen him for all of two minutes and that had been when his grandmother had blown out the candles on her cake. After that, he'd disappeared into the house and left her wondering for the umpteenth time why he'd invited her in the first place.

Moving from her spot beneath a giant pine, she started walking toward the far end of the porch where the twins were sleeping in their double stroller. A few steps away, Hannah and Bridget were engaged in a lively conversation, but both women looked around as she approached.

"Vanessa, come have a seat with us," Bridget insisted. "Hannah was just telling me what it's like at the twins' bath time."

Vanessa laughed. "I can tell you in one word. Chaos. And in a few weeks I'm sure it's going to get a lot wilder and a whole lot wetter."

She started toward an empty chair to the left of the two women, but before she reached the seat, a hand came down on the back of her shoulder. At the same time Bridget said, "Conall, it's about time you showed your face around here. Where have you been anyway?"

"Business, as usual," he answered. "A phone call I couldn't ignore. But that's finished and now I'm more than ready for a piece of cake. What about you, Vanessa?"

Turning toward him, she tried not to notice how sexy he looked in close-fitting jeans and a black T-shirt that clung to his hard torso and exposed his muscled arms. "I've already had more than my share," she told him.

"Then you can come watch me have my share," he said with a grin for her, "but first I want a look at Rose and Rick. Are they enjoying the party?"

"At least they're not howling," Hannah answered with a laugh.

He moved over to the stroller and squatted on his heels in front of the twins. Rick was asleep, his head tilted toward his sister's. But Rose was awake, her blue eyes wide, her arms pumping through the air as though she could hear the music.

"Hey, little doll, your brother is missing the party. But you'd like to dance, wouldn't you," he said in a soft voice to the baby girl. Not bothering to ask permission, he eased Rose from her side of the stroller and cradled her in the crook of his arm. Then after letting her tiny fingers curl around his forefinger, he began to slowly two-step around the porch.

"Aww, look," Bridget gushed, her gaze resting fondly on her brother and the baby in his arms. "She loves that, Conall."

"So do I," he replied with a broad grin. "I've never had a better dance partner. She's not even complaining about me stepping on her toes."

"We need him around when Rose is crying at two o'clock in the morning," Hannah joked to Vanessa.

Her eyes taking in the precious sight of Conall dancing with her daughter, Vanessa felt her throat thicken with unexpected emotions. Years ago, she'd often dreamt of Conall waltzing her around a ballroom floor. Back then she could have never imagined him holding her baby, dancing her around as though she was a special princess.

"He wouldn't be any use to you then," Bridget observed. "My brother sleeps like a rock."

Dismissing his sister's remark with a chuckle, Conall carried Rose back to the stroller. After he'd placed her back beside her brother, he pressed a kiss on her chubby cheek. "Thank you for the dance, little Rose."

To Vanessa it seemed as though he remained bent over the babies for an exceptionally long time before he finally straightened and walked back over to her. After placing his hand around

Vanessa's arm, he nodded to the other two women. "Excuse us, ladies."

He guided Vanessa off the porch and across the yard to where a table held a massive three-tiered cake and an assortment of beverages.

"Sorry I had to leave the party," he said as he gathered a plate and fork. "Have you been bored?"

"No. But I should be leaving soon. By the time Hannah and I get home with the babies, it will be getting late."

"You can't leave yet."

She watched him ladle a huge hunk of cake onto the plate. "Why? Is your family waiting to give your grandmother a surprise gift?"

"No. Kate doesn't want gifts. Says she has everything she wants. Personally, I think she needs a man in her life, but then she'd be hell to put up with, if you know what I mean."

Vanessa folded her arms against her breasts as he began to wolf down the cake. "No. I don't know what you mean. Kate might be strict and opinionated, but she wouldn't marry a man unless she loved him."

His brows lifted faintly as he looked at her. "You're probably right. She was crazy about Granddad, which always amazed me because he was a mean old cuss most of the time."

"I doubt he was mean to her. Kate is too strong of a woman to put up with that."

"Yes, but—"

"But what?"

His expression was nothing but cynical as he glanced at her. "Love makes people put up with behavior they wouldn't ordinarily tolerate."

Was he speaking from experience? Vanessa wasn't about to ask. Even though things had changed between them these past few weeks, he wasn't the type of man who poured out his personal life to anyone, including her.

Raking a hand through her hair, she looked away from him and over toward the twins. In spite of the night being pleasantly cool, she felt uncomfortably hot. "You haven't explained why I need to stay at the party a little longer," she reminded him.

He placed the now empty plate on the table and reached for her arm. "I'll explain as we walk. Let's go to Kate's rose garden. It'll be quieter there."

As the two of them disappeared into the shadows, Vanessa wondered if anyone had noticed their leaving. But why that should even matter, she didn't know. She was a grown woman and what went on between her and the manager of the Diamond D Ranch was no one's business but theirs. Yet at the same time, she had to concede that other people's opinion of her did matter. Maybe because as a poor girl growing up she'd heard the nasty whispers at school, she'd heard the gossip that Vanessa Valdez would turn out no better than her worthless brothers. And down through the years she'd worked hard to prove those people wrong, to make herself respectable and successful.

"If you needed to say something to me, you could have said it back there at the party," Vanessa told him as they trod along a graveled path that was lined with dim footlights and wound through head-high rose bushes.

"Not what I want to say."

The softness to his voice caught her attention and she paused to swing her gaze up to his shadowed face. Her heart jerked. He looked so serious, yet so sexy that her breath flew away and refused to come back.

"Conall—"

"Not here," he said. "Let's go sit in the gazebo."

Maura had told her that the gazebo had been built the same time as the huge ranch house. Now, after more than forty years, the board seats were worn smooth, along with the planked floor. A pair of aspen trees sheltered one side of the structure and as they sat down together on one of the secluded benches, the leaves rattled gently from the evening breeze.

Vanessa welcomed the cool air against her hot skin, yet it did little to chill her racing thoughts. Was he about to suggest that the two of them become lovers? That she become his mistress? She didn't know what to expect. Only one thing was clear to her—sitting in the dark with the heavenly scent of roses wrapping around them was going to be a heck of a test on her resistance.

"When my sisters were teenagers I used to tease them about sitting out here dreaming about marrying a prince or a frog. Whichever they could catch first," he said with amusement. "But after we all got older, I realized the place had a nice, calming effect. Now I think I visit the place more than they do."

"Is that why you brought me out here?" Vanessa asked wryly. "To calm me down?"

He chuckled as he reached for her hand. "That's one thing I like about you, Vanessa, you make me laugh. Something I'd almost forgotten how to do."

As his warm fingers tightened around hers,

Vanessa wasn't about to let herself think she had that much of an effect on the man. To do so would simply be dreaming. And during her doomed marriage she'd learned that a person had to be responsible for their own happiness, instead of relying on someone else to provide it for them.

She sighed. "Sometimes that's easy for a person to do—forget how to laugh." She glanced over at him, but the shadows were too deep to pick up the expression on his face. "So why are we here instead of mingling with the party guests?"

"I wanted to talk to you about…several things."

The humor was gone from his voice now and her heartbeat slowed to a heavy dread of drumbeats. "Is this about my job?" she asked.

"Actually, it is."

He'd never been evasive or short on explanations before and she wondered yet again what had brought about this change in him. Before the twins he'd been cool, work-driven and predictable. Now she couldn't begin to anticipate what he might say or do next. It was more than unnerving.

Finally, he said, "I think I need to find a different secretary."

She sucked in a sharp breath and bit down on the urge to scream at him. "You invited me to a party to fire me? Why?" she demanded. "Because I refused to make love to you?"

His lazy chuckle infuriated her.

"No. Because I've come to realize that you were right. It's too damn hard to get any work done in the office when all I want to do is lock the door and make love to you all day."

Feeling the desperate need to escape, she tried to pull her hand from his, but he held her tight, making it clear that he had plenty more to say and expected her to hang around and listen.

"Conall—"

"Wait, Vanessa, before you get all huffy, this isn't…well, it's not just about the two of us making love. It's more than that."

Confused now, she squared her knees around so that she was facing him head-on. "What *is* this about?"

He looked away from her and if Vanessa hadn't known better she would have thought he was nervous. But that couldn't be so. Conall Donovan didn't allow anything to rattle him.

Eventually he began to speak and his husky voice slid over her skin like warm, summer rain and filled her with the urge to shiver, to lean in to him and invite his kiss. She clamped her hands together and tried to concentrate on his words.

"I've been thinking about us, Vanessa. A lot. And the more I think about it the more I realize there's a perfect solution to our problem."

She swallowed as all sorts of questions raced through her head. "Problem? You mean now that you want to fire me and get another secretary?"

He grimaced. "I don't want to fire you. I mean, I do, but only because I have something different in mind—for you...for us."

Bending her head, she sucked in several deep breaths and prayed the nausea in her stomach would disappear. "Look, Conall, I like my job. I like being here on the ranch and you Donovans are excellent people to work for. But I don't appreciate the fact that you're trying to...extort sex from me! I'm not that needy. Like I told you, I can easily get a job at the casino at Ruidoso Downs and—"

"Extort sex from you! What are you talking about?"

His interruption whipped her head up. "Why, yes, isn't that what this is all about? You want me to quit my job and be your mistress?"

With a groan of disbelief, he clasped his

hands over both her shoulders. "Oh, Vanessa, I'm sorry. I must be doing this all wrong. I don't want you to be my mistress. I want you to be my wife."

Chapter Eight

If he'd not been holding on to her, Vanessa was sure she would have fallen straight backward and onto the floor of the gazebo.

"Your wife!" she said in a shocked whisper. "Are you…out of your mind?"

There was no smile on his face, no glimmer that he was anywhere near teasing.

"Not in the least. The twins need a father. And you and I…well, we obviously get on together. I think it's the perfect solution for all of us."

Stunned, she rose to her feet and walked to the other side of the gazebo. In her wildest imaginings, she'd not expected this from

Conall. Twenty years ago, when she'd viewed him as a knight on horseback, she'd fantasized how it would be to receive a kiss from him, or even go on a date with him, but even her fantasies had known when and where to stop. Men like Conall didn't marry women like her.

She heard his footsteps approaching her from behind and then his hands came to rest upon her shoulders. As their warmth seeped into her skin, she closed her eyes and wondered why she suddenly wanted to weep.

"Vanessa, what are you thinking?"

Her throat was aching, making her voice low and strained. "I'm...very flattered, Conall. But marriage needs to be more than a solution."

His sigh rustled the top of her hair. "I'm trying to be practical, Vanessa. Marriage—making a family together—would be good for all four of us."

Maybe it would, she thought sadly, but what about love? He'd not mentioned the word, but then he hardly needed to explain his feelings. She already understood that he didn't love her.

Turning, she demanded, "How would it be good for you, Conall?"

His arms slipped around her waist and drew the front of her body up against his. "Just having you next to me would be good," he murmured.

She groaned as a war of wanting him and needing his love erupted inside of her. "I'm sorry, Conall, but it hasn't been that long since I got out of a horrible marriage. I don't want to jump into something that...well, I'm just not sure about."

He frowned. "Do you think I'm taking this whole thing lightly? That I proposed to you on impulse? Hell, Vanessa, my marriage turned out to be a nightmare. For a while after the divorce I tried to date again, to find a woman I could build a relationship with. But the past refused to let that happen so I finally gave up trying. So if you think you're the only one who has a corner on being hurt by a spouse, then think again."

"That's exactly why this is all so crazy!" she exclaimed. "Why would you want to marry a divorced woman with two newborns when..."

"Finish what you were going to say, Vanessa. When...?"

Pressing her lips together, she looked away from him. Through the lattice covering the side of the gazebo, she could see the lights of the party twinkling through the pine boughs. Shrieks of laughter were coming from the pool and closer to the house she could hear several voices singing "Happy Birthday" to Kate. The fact that Conall had chosen this night to propose to her while his family was celebrating seemed surreal.

Biting back an impatient curse, she turned away from him. "Don't play dumb with me, Conall. It doesn't suit you at all. You know what I was about to say. You're a Donovan. You don't have to go around looking for a woman to marry. All you have to do is get the word out and they'll come running to you. You certainly don't have to settle for your secretary."

His face stony, he caught her by the shoulder and spun her back around. "Why are you doing your best to insult me and yourself? Me being a Donovan has nothing to do with us marrying!"

Amazed, her head swung back and forth. "Conall, that's a fact that can't be buried or swept under the rug!"

His nostrils flared. "Why do you think so little of yourself?"

Tears were suddenly burning her eyes. "Because...oh, you can't understand anything, can you? I've already had one husband who didn't love me! Do you honestly think I want another?"

Before he could answer, she twisted away from him and dashed out of the gazebo. As she hurried along the lighted footpaths, she did her best to stem the hot moisture threatening to spill onto her cheeks.

She'd made a fool of herself, she thought bitterly. Of course, Conall couldn't understand her reaction to his proposal. He couldn't know that she loved him and, perhaps, had always loved him. She was just now beginning to realize that herself.

At one time in his life, long before he'd learned of his sterility, Conall had been comfortable with women. As very young men, Liam had struggled to converse with the opposite sex, while Conall had instinctively known exactly what to say or do to make a woman adore him. Long before he'd met Nancy, he'd dated a lengthy list of beauties and he could safely say that each of the relationships had eventually ended on his terms, not his partner's. Whether his success with women had been partly due to his being a Donovan was a question he'd not considered that much. Until last night when Vanessa had flung the fact in his face.

Obviously he'd lost his touch. Or maybe the long marriage battle he'd endured with Nancy had taken away his innate ability to deal with a woman. Whatever the reason, he'd clearly done everything wrong when he'd proposed to Vanessa last night.

Glancing at his watch, he noted it was a quarter to eight. Normally Vanessa had arrived by now. Especially on a Monday. But he'd not heard any stirrings in the outer office and he was beginning to wonder if she'd decided to skip work altogether today. Or maybe she was going to quit and was planning to call and let the gavel drop on him.

Thrusting fingers through his dark hair, he pressed fingertips against his scalp. Tiny men were pounding sledgehammers just beneath his skull, a result of drinking too many beers last night after Vanessa had taken the babies and gone home, he thought grimly. He'd never been one to indulge in alcohol, but after the fiasco in the gazebo, he needed some sort of relief. Now he was paying for it with a doozy of a headache.

A hard knock on the doorjamb had him

wincing and he glanced around to see Liam striding into his office.

"What's with all the roses in Vanessa's office? Did someone break into a florist shop this morning or something?" he asked.

With an awkward shrug, Conall admitted, "I broke into Grandma's rose garden. I knew it would be useless to drive to town and try to bribe a shop owner to open up and deliver this morning."

His brows arched with curiosity, Liam glanced over his shoulder toward the outer office. "I didn't realize your secretary was that important to you. What is today, secretary's day or something? If it is, Gloria is out of luck."

Conall grunted. "The only thing Gloria ever expects from you is win photos to put on the wall behind her desk."

"That's all?" he countered with sarcasm. "It would be a hell of a lot easier to raid Grandma's flower garden and blame it on the gardener."

Conall walked over to the coffeepot and refilled his mug. "Coffee?" he asked his brother.

"No. I'm in a hurry. I'm missed you at breakfast, so I wanted to let you know I was ship-

ping Red Garland to Del Mar today, along with
a few others."

He looked around at Liam. "To Del Mar?
Now?"

Liam rolled his eyes with impatience. "Have
you forgotten she's entered in the Debutante?
That's only a month away and I want her to
get accustomed to the Pacific climate and the
Polytrack before race time."

Actually it had slipped Conall's mind that
the filly would be traveling to the west coast to
run in the prestigious race at one of the most
famous tracks in California. "Sorry, brother, I
guess the time has slipped up on me."

"Geez, Conall. What's going on with you?
From the moment she was born Red Garland
has always been your darling. And you've forgotten about her first stakes debut?"

Conall had been in the foaling barn, watching when Red Garland entered the world. Only
hours later, the baby girl had left her mother's
side to investigate Conall's outstretched hand
and something about her trust had touched
him, had gotten to him in a way no human
ever had. Since then, she'd grown up to be an
outstanding runner that had quickly stunned
race fans with her ability to outdistance herself
from the rest of the pack. Conall was extremely

proud of her. He was also very attached to the filly. Something he normally didn't allow himself to be with the horses they raised and raced.

Conall glanced at his brother's incredulous expression. "Maybe you haven't noticed but I've had a lot going on here lately," he said, then shoved out a heavy breath. "Anyway, I'm glad you came by to say you were leaving. I... well, I'll be honest, I hate for her to be shipped all the way to California."

Liam frowned. "Why? We ship horses out there all the time."

Conall felt like a soppy idiot. "I know. It's just that...anything might happen. That Polytrack surface is unpredictable."

"So is the dirt."

"She might hurt herself. With an injury that could end her career or even kill her," Conall pointed out, even though both men were already well aware of that fact. "But you're the trainer. You know what she can handle best."

Liam shook his head. "Hell, Conall. You're my brother. I don't want to do anything against your wishes."

With a self-effacing grunt, Conall placed his coffee mug on the edge of the desk. "What's the matter with me, Liam? I've never gotten this soppy over any of our horses before. I've never let myself. Because...well, we both know anything can happen to lose them."

"Sometimes something or someone comes along to remind us we're not machines," Liam said thoughtfully, then added, "I'll scratch Red Garland from the Debutante and leave her here. We'll lose the entry fee, but what the hell. She's already won that much a thousand times over."

"No, she's going," Conall said with sudden firmness. "She deserves her chance to be great."

A wry smile touched Liam's lips. "Well, she stands a good chance to win a pile of money."

"Yeah. But money isn't everything," Conall replied.

Liam grunted in agreement. "Sometimes it doesn't mean anything at all."

Satisfied that things were settled with the situation, Liam turned to leave the room, but before he disappeared out the door, Conall called to him, "Thanks, again, Liam. For coming by and reminding me about Red Garland's race. Will you be following the horses out today or tomorrow?"

"Today and I'm taking three grooms with me."

Conall lifted his hand in farewell. "Travel safely and I'll see you when you get back."

"You want to drive to the airport and see Red Garland off this afternoon?" Liam asked in an afterthought.

"No. I'd rather meet her there when she gets back."

With a nod of understanding, Liam left the office and Conall forced himself to sit down at his desk.

Five minutes later, he heard the outer door to the office open and close and then Vanessa's light footsteps cross the tile. Normally, she went straight to the closet they shared to store away her purse and whatever sort of wrap she was wearing but so far the closet hadn't opened.

He forced himself to wait another minute before he walked through the open door and into her section of the office. He found her standing in front of the desk, staring at the massive vase of pink roses he'd left for her.

Upon hearing his approach, she whirled around to face him. "What are these?"

Conall walked toward her. "Roses. To say I'm sorry if I hurt you last night. I didn't mean to. I didn't have any idea a marriage proposal would be so harrowing to you."

Bending her head, she closely examined the petals on the tea roses. "I'll be honest, Conall,

I considered not coming to work this morning. But I didn't want Fiona to have to fill in for me. So I made myself drive over here." Turning slightly, she leveled her brown eyes on him. "I'm sorry, too, Conall. I overreacted about you—about everything. I was expecting too much from you. I realize that now."

Relieved that she no longer appeared angry, he walked over to her. "I'm glad you're here," he confessed. "And if you don't want to talk about things right now, we won't."

Her glaze flickered away from his face and back to the roses and Conall was struck by how very beautiful she looked this morning. Her hair was swept up and off her neck, while a heavy fringe fell in a smooth curtain over one eyebrow. Her dress was white, the neckline fashioned in a deep V. Faint freckles dotted her chest and lower down a hint of cleavage teased his senses. The pale pink color on her lips reminded him of a seashell and he realized he'd like nothing better than to kiss the shimmery color away, kiss her until her lips were ruby-red and swollen.

"There's nothing to talk about," she said wearily. "I can't marry you."

Desperate to touch her, he planted his hands on either side of her waist. "Listen, Vanessa, I have no idea what happened in your marriage or what kind of man your husband was, but please don't compare me to him."

To his surprise she laughed with disbelief. "Oh, Conall, you can't imagine how…well, how opposite you are from Jeff. He didn't have an ounce of ambition. He was perfectly content to let me support him."

Trying to understand, he shook his head. "I'm guessing you didn't know this about him before you married?"

Grimacing, she stepped away from him. "Of course I didn't! When I first met him he was doing contract electrical work for the casino where I was employed. At that time he owned a small building company and he and his men had more jobs than they could handle. He made very good money, plus he was from a nice respectable family that had resided in Bullhead City for many years. There was nothing about Jeff that warned he would turn out to be a deadhead."

She started into his office and Conall followed her to the coffee machine. As she poured herself a mug and stirred in a measure of half-and-half, he couldn't stop himself from asking, "When did you learn he was less than ambitious?"

Cradling the mug with both hands, she turned to face him. "About six months after we were married. He began to find all sorts of reasons not to take jobs. Mainly he would use the excuse that he wanted to spend more time with me—because I was so irresistible he didn't want to leave me for a minute of the day," she added with sarcasm. "Dear God, was I ever stupid to believe his lines. But he…well, he had a charming, lovable way about him that was hard to resist and I—" Pausing, she shook her head with self-reproach. "I guess he'd come along in my life at a time when I was feeling very alone. My brothers were long gone and I was watching my parents grow old. I wanted a family of my own and Jeff kept promising we'd have one. I hung on hoping and praying he'd change. But in the end, I think all he ever wanted was to have fun and a woman to take care of him while he was having it. I should have seen that from the very beginning, but I didn't. And it's taken me a long time to convince myself that I'm not a fool. That I'm worthy of better than…him."

The faint quiver Conall heard in her voice touched a spot in him that he'd long thought dead and he was amazed at how much he wanted to take her into his arms, to whisper

how beautiful and precious she was to him.
Did that mean he loved her? No. It couldn't
mean that. He'd forgotten how to love. But he'd
not forgotten how to want and he wanted Vanessa in his life. He wanted to be a father to
Rick and Rose.

I wanted a family of my own.

Her words had pierced him right in the heart
and twisted home the reality of his condition,
his failed marriage and the total emptiness he'd
carried inside him for all these years. Maybe he
should confess to her right now that he couldn't
father a child. But she was already reluctant to
trust him, to believe they could have a good
marriage together. He didn't want to wham her
with that kind of revelation. She would automatically think he was only interested in the
twins. Later, he told himself. Later, after he'd
convinced her to marry him, he would explain
it all. He would make her understand just how
perfect the four of them were for each other.

"Oh, Vanessa," he said lowly, "you are worthy of better. And I like to think I can give
you better."

Her gaze dropped awkwardly to the brown
liquid in her cup. "Yes, you could give me better in so many ways," she conceded. "Except
you can't give me what I need the most."

She sounded so defeated, so sure, and that worried Conall more than any words she could have said to him.

"What is that?" he asked.

She looked up at him and he spotted a mixture of defiance and resignation swimming in the depths of her brown eyes.

"Love."

The one word caused Conall to rear back and unwittingly drop his hands from her waist. "Love," he repeated, rolling the word around on his tongue as if he'd never spoken it before. "You mentioned that word last night, but you didn't give me a chance to have my say on the matter."

"All right," she said in a faintly challenging tone. "I'm giving you the chance right now."

Finding it difficult to face her head-on, Conall moved away from her and over to the huge plate glass window overlooking the stables. "And I'm telling you right now that love is a fairy-tale state of mind. That's all. It's just a euphoric condition that doesn't last. In fact, it only makes living with a person worse."

Her light footsteps sounded behind him and he turned to see she'd joined him at the window, but she wasn't looking out at the busy shed row, she was looking at him with so much disappointment that she might as well have struck him physically.

"No wonder your marriage crumbled."

Now, a voice inside his head shouted, *now is the time to explain everything, to defend yourself and your actions.* But he couldn't push the words off his tongue. She was already looking at him with disenchantment; he didn't want to add even more to it.

The tiny hammers pounding at his skull grew harder and he wiped a hand over his face in hopes of easing the pain. "I loved Nancy when we married," he said with gruff insistence. "And I loved her for a long time afterward. But love can't hold up to life's interventions. At least, it didn't for me."

She didn't reply and he used her silence as an opportunity to plead his case. Latching a hand over her shoulder, he pressed his fingers into her warm flesh. "Think about it, Vanessa. Love didn't give your marriage a happily-ever-after ending. Nor did it mine. But you and I have the chance to build a marriage on a solid foundation. Not something that crumbles at the slightest hint of trouble."

Her nostrils flared with disdain as she drew in a deep breath and let it out. "I've never heard of anything so...unfeeling," she muttered.

Before she could guess his intentions, he took the mug from her hands and placed it on the wide window ledge.

"There is nothing unfeeling about this, Vanessa. Maybe I ought to show you."

Pulling her into his arms, he fastened his lips roughly over hers. A moan sounded in her throat at the same time her mouth opened like flower petals seeking the hot sun. His tongue thrust past her teeth and began to explore the sweet, moist contours.

With his hands at her back, he pulled her closer, until her small breasts were flattened against his chest, until he felt the mound of her womanhood pressing into his thigh. Heat was rushing through him, gorging his loins with the unbearable need to get inside her. His sex was rock-hard and pushing against the fly of his jeans.

He couldn't remember the last time, if ever, he'd wanted a woman like this, and when her arms slid around his waist and her soft body arched into his, it was all he could do to hang on to his self-control, to lift his head and speak.

"Let me go lock the door," he said hoarsely.

His words must have hit her like a cold wall of water. Jerking away from him, she stumbled backward and pressed a hand against her throat. "No! You've made your point, Conall. You want me physically. And I admit I want you. But that's not enough. I'm not going to let it be enough. Not now. Not again."

She started toward the door and though Conall wanted to go after her, he realized it wasn't the time or the place to press her. But, oh, God, he desperately wanted to.

"I'm going to work," she said over her shoulder. "If that isn't enough for you, then hire yourself another secretary!"

He stood where he was until the door between their offices shut firmly behind her. Once it was obvious she wasn't going to reappear or change her mind, Conall stalked over to his desk and sank into the lush leather chair.

Damn, damn, damn. What would it take to make her cozy up to the idea of marrying him? Or would she ever come around to his way of thinking? She wanted love, but how could he give her the one thing he didn't have?

With a frustrated oath, he picked up the phone and punched in Liam's cell number. His brother answered after the third ring.

"Yeah. What's up?"

"I...just wanted to see what time the plane with the horses would be departing the airport."

"Probably around eleven this morning. Why?"

Pinching the bridge of his nose, Conall closed his eyes. "I've changed my mind. I've decided I want to see Red Garland off."

Liam grunted. "What's brought this on?" he asked bluntly.

Conall grimaced. "Do I have to explain myself?" he countered gruffly. "Maybe I want to see her one last time. In case...she doesn't come home."

The line went silent for long moments, then Liam gently cursed, "Hell, Conall. I promise I'll bring the filly back."

"You can't make promises like that." He swallowed hard and glanced at the closed door between him and Vanessa. "Don't let the plane leave until I get there."

The next two days Vanessa was bombarded with an extra flurry of work while Conall was continually tied up with issues both in and out of the office. She'd done her best to deal with tractor dealers, feed suppliers and tack salesmen even as she plowed through mounds of paperwork.

Being busier than usual was a good thing, she supposed. That gave her less time to dwell on Conall. Since that fiery kiss they'd exchanged, they'd been polite and civil to each other, but the words and the touches they'd exchanged had hung in the air between them like a heavy humidity, leaving Vanessa uncomfortable and emotionally drained.

At the end of the second day, Vanessa was sitting at her desk, finishing a phone call and wrapping up her work for the evening, when Conall strolled through the door and eased a hip onto the edge of her desk. After two days of tiptoeing around each other, his casual nearness jolted her.

Looking up at him, she asked briskly, "Is there something you need?"

"I need a lot of things, but I won't have you make a list now." He gestured toward her work. "Are you nearly finished?"

"Yes. As soon as I make a few notes in my message book. Why?"

The faint grin on his face was the warmest thing she'd seen since the morning he'd wanted to lock the two of them in his office and his gray eyes had been hot with lust. She had to wonder about the abrupt change.

Folding his arms against his chest, his expression turned sheepish. "I wanted to see if you've forgiven me enough to have dinner with me this evening?"

Forgiven him? She'd not been expecting anything like this. Maybe a request for her to work later than usual, but not anything sociable, like having dinner together.

"You've been all business the past couple of days," she bluntly pointed out.

"So have you."

Her gaze dropped from his face to the vase of roses he'd given her a few days ago. She should have thrown them out or at least taken them home and given them to Hannah. But they were still as pretty as the morning she'd found them on her desk and she couldn't bring herself to get rid of them.

When she didn't reply, he said, "I thought we both needed some time to cool off."

That was an understatement, Vanessa thought wryly. Her gaze flickered back up to his face. "And you think we've *cooled off* enough to have dinner together? Alone?"

"We've eaten together alone before," he reminded, as if her memory needed refreshing. "At your house. And in Vegas."

She sighed. He'd been so sweet, so helpful during that trip to Las Vegas and for as long as she lived, she would never forget the look on his face when he'd held the twins for the first time. He'd looked at them with affection and tenderness and for those few moments she'd seen the part of him that she admired, wanted, loved.

"I remember," she told him.

"I'd like to do it again. Would you?"

She'd be lying if she told him no. These past couple of days as she'd kept her distance, she'd constantly argued with herself that it was better that way. The only thing she could ever expect to get from the man was sex. Yet even knowing that hadn't been enough to stop the hunger inside of her, the need to be near him in all the ways a woman could be near a man.

"Yes," she answered. "But—"

"What? Afraid you might find out that you like me after all?"

In spite of her torn emotions, she chuckled. "Oh, Conall, you know that I like you. Very much. That's the whole problem." She closed the small book where she scribbled down daily notes and stuffed it away in the top drawer of the desk. "We... Well, I'm not going to go into any of that tonight. Going out with you is out of the question. I've already promised my father I'd visit him after I got off work. And I'm not going to disappoint him for any reason."

"I wouldn't want you to disappoint him. We'll go by and visit him together," he said.

While she looked at him her thoughts swirled. "He's in the nursing home."

"I'm well aware of that, Vanessa."

Jeff would have never stepped foot in a nursing home, she thought. Not for anyone. In that way he'd been a thoughtless man. Unfortunately, she'd learned about Jeff's unpleasant traits after they'd been married, a fault she could only place squarely on herself. She'd been so eager to be loved, so anxious to be a wife and mother, that she'd been blinded by Jeff's charms and his quick press for them to marry.

With a mental sigh, she did her best to shove away the dark memories before she glanced down at the simple wrap dress she was wearing. The pale green geometric print still looked fresh enough, but it wasn't exactly what she would have picked to wear for a date with Conall. A date? If that's what this was supposed to be then he was going backward, she thought. Dates were supposed to come before marriage proposals, not after. But then she could hardly forget that Conall's proposal had not been the conventional sort, where a man promised his love for a lifetime.

"We can't go anywhere fancy," she finally said. "I'm not dressed for it."

He reached over and plucked one of the dark pink roses from the bouquet he'd given her. "You are now," he murmured as he tucked the flower behind her left ear. "A rose in your hair to match the roses on your cheeks."

Clearing her tight throat, she said, "I didn't know you could flirt."

He grinned. "I'll be happy to show you what else I can do."

Forbidden images raced through her mind. "I'll go get my handbag so we can be going."

Rising from the chair, she purposefully moved away from him and the desk before she lost all sense and reached for him, before she could tell him that the only place she wanted to go was straight into his arms.

Chapter Nine

A few minutes later they were traveling toward Ruidoso in Conall's plush black truck. Only moments ago they'd watched the sun slip behind the mountains, and now in the western sky rich magenta threads laced together a cloak of purple clouds.

Being cooped up in the cozy cab with Conall was a temptation in itself and so far she'd been doing her best to concentrate on the scenery instead of his long, lean presence. But since they'd departed the ranch, he'd been in a surprisingly talkative mood and she'd found her gaze lingering on him far more than it should have.

"How long has Alonzo been in the nursing home?" he asked as he capably maneuvered the truck over the steeply winding highway.

Back at the office, he'd tugged a black cowboy hat low on his forehead and now as Vanessa glanced at his profile, she could only think that this man was living his days out not really in the way he wanted, but as he thought he was expected to. As a teenager she'd spent enough time on the ranch to see that Conall had been an outdoorsman, a horseman. She sensed that deep down, he would much rather be working hands-on with the horses than dealing with business issues. But apparently he considered managing the ranch his family duty and from what she could tell about the man, Conall would never shun his family responsibilities. In that aspect, he would be an excellent husband and father. But did duty mean more than love? Not to her.

"About six months," she answered. "After his stroke he was in the hospital for nearly a month before he was well enough to go to the nursing home. He's doing much better now, but he still has a way to go. I've hired a speech therapist to work with him and that's made a great difference. He's actually beginning to talk again with words that are understandable."

He nodded. "Do you think he'll ever get to come home?"

"If he continues to improve, his doctor says it's highly possible. But he'll not be able to live alone." She sighed. "I'm hoping when, or maybe I should say if, that happens, the twins won't be so demanding of me."

Chuckling lowly, he shook his head. "I'm sorry, Vanessa, but I don't think it's going to work that way. I have a feeling that the older the twins get, the more they're going to demand of their mother. Especially since—"

He broke off as though he had second thoughts about his next words. Vanessa didn't press him. She simply waited.

"Well," he finally said, "no matter about the twins. I'm sure you'd love to have your father well again and back home. If it was my father, I certainly would."

She smiled wanly. "More than anything. He's all alone. And I have a feeling the twins would be good for him."

"The twins are very special," he said with undisguised warmth. "But you would be good for him, too. You have a way of making people around you feel better about themselves."

With a shake of her head, she said, "You don't have to overdo it, Conall."

He mouthed a curse under his breath. "I'm not overdoing anything, Vanessa. If you... Well, you've made me realize that divorcing Nancy didn't make me a criminal or a devil. Nor did it end my life."

Curiosity sparked in her and she couldn't stop herself from asking, "You were the one who wanted the divorce?"

He grimaced. "Yes," he answered bluntly.

"Why?"

Sighing, he said, "We had fundamental differences in what we thought was important to our lives and our marriage. But in the end she...betrayed me in a way that was unforgivable."

Had Nancy cheated on Conall with another man? She'd never met the woman who'd once been in the Donovan family, but she found it hard to imagine her committing adultery on a man that was breathtakingly sexy, unless the cheating had been more about her unhappiness. "You don't believe in forgiveness?" she asked.

A wry twist to his lips, he said, "I can forgive, Vanessa. But forgiving wouldn't have fixed the problem."

"Oh."

He looked at her. "Let's not waste this evening talking about such things. It's in the past and that's where it's going to stay. So tell me some of your favorite foods and we'll decide where to eat."

He obviously wanted to change the subject and Vanessa could understand why. She didn't particularly enjoy talking about Jeff and the mistakes she made with him. No doubt Conall felt the same.

"All right," she agreed, "I like anything I can eat with my hands. How about a hamburger?"

He flashed her a grin. "I knew we'd be perfect together. You just proved it."

Groaning inwardly, Vanessa could have told him there wasn't such a thing as being perfect together. Maybe for a few minutes at a time, but not for a lifetime. But she kept the cynical thought to herself. Now that she'd agreed to spend the evening with Conall, she didn't want to spoil their time together with more useless arguments.

Once they reached town, Vanessa started to give Conall directions to the nursing home, but he quickly interrupted.

"I know where it is, Vanessa. I've been there many times."

She looked at him with surprise. "I didn't realize any of your family had been incapacitated. From what Maura's told me, your grandfather's death was rather quick."

"I've not had a family member living in Gold Aspen Manor. But Liam's assistant stayed there until…his death."

By now they had reached the one-story, ranch-style building that sat in a carved out area of a wooded foothill. Slanted parking slots skirted a wide front lawn where sprinklers were going and a gardener was meticulously edging the sidewalk. It was a quiet and beautiful place, but Vanessa cringed each time she walked through the doors. She wanted her father to be whole and well again. She wanted him to be back on his little patch of land, scratching out a small garden and tending his goats.

"I didn't realize Liam ever had an assistant," she admitted. "I took it for granted that he'd always worked alone."

Conall cut the motor, but didn't make any hurried moves to depart the truck. "No. Before Liam was experienced enough to take on the task of being head trainer, Cletis—we called him Clete—was the man. He mentored Liam, then after handing the reins over to him, continued to work alongside my brother until about three years ago when his health began to fail. Liam's not been the same since the old man passed away."

"I can understand that. I've not been the same since my mother passed," Vanessa sadly admitted. "Everything that once was important to me now looks so different, almost trivial."

His expression suddenly sober, he let out a long breath. "Yeah. Well, Clete didn't have a family. He regarded Liam as a son. And Liam doesn't think anyone could ever fill Clete's boots. That's mainly why he continues to work himself to death instead of hiring a new assistant." With a wry expression, he reached over and touched her hand. "Come on, that's enough about that stuff. Let's go see your father."

To Vanessa's delight they found Alonzo outside, seated around a patio table with a group of men who were also patients at the Gold Aspen Manor. As soon as the older man spotted her approach, he rose from his chair and held out his arms to her.

Leaving Conall's side, she rushed to her father and hugged him tight. After he'd kissed both her cheeks, he put her away from him with a strength that surprised her.

"Wow, you're awfully spry this evening," she said with a happy laugh. "What have they been feeding you around here, spinach?"

Alonzo's dark wrinkled face split into a grin for his daughter. "Can't stand that stuff. Meat. Fresh meat. That's what's done it."

Pressing her cheek against his, she hugged him once again, before gesturing toward Conall, who was standing a few steps behind her. "I brought someone with me tonight, Dad. You remember Conall?"

The old man's brown eyes flickered with surprise, quickly followed by pleasure. "Sure, sure. Donovan. That right?"

Smiling, Conall stepped forward and reached to shake her father's hand. "That's exactly right, Mr. Valdez. It's good to see you again."

The other man nodded with approval. "Good to see you. Yes."

Looping her arm through his, Vanessa asked, "Do you think you can make it over to that empty table where we can sit down and talk?"

To her surprise, he pushed away her helping hand. "Show you. Watch," he said proudly.

Moving aside, she stood next to Conall and watched as Alonzo walked slowly but surely the twenty-foot distance to the empty table.

"Your father looks like he's doing great to me," Conall said under his breath.

She glanced up at him with pleased wonder. "I've never seen his back so straight and he's actually lifting his feet and putting them down instead of shuffling. He's improved so much from just a week ago."

Giving the side of her waist an encouraging squeeze, he inclined his head toward Alonzo. "Let's join him."

For the next forty minutes the three of them talked about the twins, then on to several local happenings, until finally the two men began to reminisce about the time Alonzo restored one of the Diamond D horse barns. Vanessa hadn't been aware that her father had ever contracted work for the Donovans or that he'd known the family so personally. But that didn't begin to describe the shock she felt when Conall suddenly scooted his chair close to Vanessa's and curled his arm around her shoulders in a completely possessive way.

"Alonzo, has your daughter told you that I've asked her to marry me?"

The old man appeared stunned and then he turned accusing eyes upon his daughter. "She did not tell me."

Conall shot her a devilish smile. "Why haven't you told your father about us?"

It was all Vanessa could do to stop herself

from kicking his shins beneath the table. "Because it—" Jerking her eyes off Conall's expectant face, she looked over to her father. "Because I told him no!"

Alonzo studied her closely. "Why?"

"Yeah, why?" Conall echoed the older man's question.

She wanted to kill the man for putting her on the spot like this in front of her father. And yet, a part of her felt ridiculously warm and wanted and a bit like a princess to have Conall Donovan declaring to her father that he wanted to marry her.

"Because I—" She turned a challenging look on Conall. "I want a husband who will love me."

Alonzo's sharp gaze leveled on Conall and then after a moment he chuckled. The sound didn't just stun Vanessa, it also angered her.

"That'll come," Alonzo said with beaming confidence. "Later."

Jumping to her feet, she tugged on Conall's arm. "We've got to be going. Now!"

Conall didn't argue and after she gave her father a quick goodbye, the two of them hurried around to a side exit of the building and on to the parked truck.

As he helped her climb into the cab, she

hissed under her breath, "What the hell were you doing back there?"

"Telling Alonzo my intentions toward his daughter," he answered easily. "As far as I'm concerned, that's the respectable thing for a man to do."

"But you did it on purpose!"

"Of course I did it on purpose." As she settled herself in the seat, he shut the door and rounded the truck. Once he was under the wheel and starting the engine, he said, "I don't say things just to be saying them, Vanessa."

Groaning helplessly, she swiped a hand across her forehead. "Now Dad is going to be wondering about us and expecting—"

"What?"

"Me to marry you. That's what. He likes and respects you and he's been telling me that I need a husband. It's all simple logic to him."

Conall smiled. "He did appear pleased about the whole thing. But I always did think your father was a wise man."

Latching on to his last words, she jerked her head around to stare at him in wonder. "You never cease to surprise me, Conall."

"Why?" he asked with a puzzled frown. "What have I done now?"

Suddenly her heart was melting like candy

clutched in a warm palm. Maybe he didn't love her outright, but he was good in so many other ways that she was beginning to wonder if she was crazy for refusing to marry him. "Nothing. You complimented my father. Did you really mean that when you called him wise?"

He backed the truck onto the street and directed it down the steep street. "Like I said, I don't say things just to be saying them. Your dad has weathered plenty of storms and he's done it without bending or begging. He's worked hard all his life and managed to hold his land and his home together. That takes wisdom." He glanced at her. "Plus he knew how to keep your mother happy. I could see that each time I saw them together in church. They looked at each other the same way my parents look at each other."

She swallowed hard as emotions thickened her throat. "You mean...with love?"

His features tightened ever so slightly. "I'd rather call it respect."

Vanessa couldn't argue that respect was a key ingredient in a marriage. But it wasn't enough to keep her heart warm and full. It didn't thrill her or fill her with hunger or need or joy.

"By all means call it that if it makes you feel

safer," Vanessa told him as she unconsciously reached up and touched the rose he'd placed above her ear. "I prefer to call it what it is."

They ate at a tiny café on the northwest side of town called the Sugar Shack, in tribute to the decadent homemade desserts that were served there. Over the casual dinner, all mention of love and marriage, or anything close to it, was avoided by both of them and eventually Vanessa was able to relax and enjoy the good food.

Once the meal was over and they exited the building, she pressed a hand to her stomach and groaned. "I've not eaten that much in ages. I'll probably have nightmares tonight after stuffing myself."

"I have a perfect place for you to walk some of that meal off," he suggested slyly.

Spend more time with this man? Alone? The sane, sensible and smart thing for her to do would be go straight home. He made her crazy and on edge, yet at the same time he made her undeniably happy. She was at a loss as to how to deal with the contradictory feelings, especially when a part of her was screaming to simply give up and give in to her desires.

"I really should get back home and give Hannah some relief."

He moved his arm around the back of her waist and guided her toward the truck. "I promise you, Hannah and the twins can make it without you for a little while longer. And if you don't feel like doing any walking, we can always do a little stargazing."

Her mouth opened to utter another protest, but that was as far as her resistance would take her. "All right," she conceded. "It would be nice to stay out a little longer."

"That's exactly what I was thinking."

Once they were back in the truck, he drove northwest until most of the town was behind them. After turning onto a narrow dirt road, they wound upward through a tall stand of pines and spruce trees until they were near the crest of the mountain. Just when she'd decided he was probably taking her to a state campground, the road ended and the forest opened up. Beyond the beam of headlights she could see some sort of house constructed of cedar wood and native rock.

"Is this your place?" she asked as he parked the truck near a big blue spruce.

"It belongs to the Diamond D," he answered. "We have guests, horse buyers, or out-of-town friends fly in to attend the races and this place is a lot closer to the track than the ranch. Our city friends especially enjoy the privacy." He reached to release his seat belt. "Let's get out and I'll show you around."

Once he helped Vanessa down from the truck, he took a firm hold on her hand. "Be careful and watch your step," he warned as they started toward the house. "Dad doesn't want to install a yard light up here. Says it would ruin the effect. So at night it's dark as hell."

"The moon is rising," she remarked as she cast an observing glance at the eastern sky. "That gives us walking light."

The back part of the structure sat on the edge of the mountainside, while the front was supported with huge wooden pillars. She figured the Donovans considered this a mere mountain cabin, but to regular folks like her it was more like an opulent getaway.

The two of them climbed long steps up to a wide planked deck that also served as a porch. Conall led her over to the far end and they leaned against a waist-high wooden railing to gaze beyond the surrounding forest to a majestic view of the valley below.

"It's beautiful up here!" she said with quiet wonder.

He said, "Well, you can't exactly get the full effect of the view in the moonlight, but we'll come back again when the sun is out and the weather is nice. You'll really appreciate it then."

His suggestion implied that he planned to spend more personal time with her. The idea thrilled her, yet troubled her. No doubt the more time she spent with him, the more she would fall in love with him. And where would that eventually leave her? Loving a man who was unable to love her in return?

No. She didn't want to think about that right now. Since her divorce more than a year ago, she'd kept a high fence around herself. Before she'd taken even the tiniest of steps, she'd stopped and looked in all four directions to make sure she wasn't about to be waylaid by something or someone. Careful, cautious and controlled, that was how she'd lived her life since her marriage had ended. Now she was struck with the reckless urge to break free of those cold boundaries, to let herself live and feel again. No matter the painful consequences.

Sighing, she turned toward him. "I'm glad you asked me out tonight," she admitted.

His smile was full of doubt. "That's hard to believe. I haven't exactly been one of your favorite people since...well, since that morning at the office when I wanted to make love to you."

The memory of that incident still had the power to heat her cheeks and she was grateful the darkness masked the telltale color on her cheeks. "Make love to me? Don't you mean you wanted to have sex with me?"

In the silver moonlight she could see a grimace cross his face. "I was trying to be tactful. Making love sounds better."

"I'd prefer honesty over sounding nice." She directed her gaze away from his face to a dark corner of the deck. "Actually, I should tell you that I was angrier at myself that day than I was with you."

His hand released hers only to wrap around her upper arm. Since her dress was sleeveless, the feel of his fingers against her bare skin was like throwing drops of water into a hot skillet. The sizzle vibrated all the way down to her toes.

He said, "I don't understand."

She dared to look up at his shadowed face.

"You should understand, Conall. It's not smart of me to want you. But I do," she added in a whisper.

Suddenly the hand that had been burning a ring around her arm slid upward until his long fingers were curved against her throat. No doubt he could feel the hammering of her pulse and knew exactly what his touch was doing to her. But then, he'd probably always known how weak and utterly helpless he made her.

"You shouldn't have been angry with either one of us," he murmured. "And if it's honesty you want, I can truthfully say I want you, Vanessa. More than I've ever wanted any woman."

From any other man, a trite line like that would have garnered a groan of disgust from Vanessa, but coming from Conall she wanted to believe it was uttered with sincerity. Oh, yes, to think he desired her over any other woman was more than a heady thought. But thinking, wondering, deciding what was right or wrong was quickly taking a backseat. Instead of her brain, her heart had taken control and it was urging her body to press against his, begging her arms to wrap around his waist.

"Don't say any more, Conall. Just show me."

She heard him suck in a sharp breath and then his lips were suddenly hovering over hers.

"Vanna. Vanna."

The repeated whisper of her nickname was like a warm, sweet caress and she sighed ever so slightly before his lips latched on to hers, his hands slid to the small of her back and pressed her body into his.

She'd expected his kiss to be a lazy, searching seduction, but it was anything but. His lips were rampaging over hers, taking her breath and searing her senses with the depth of his desire. She tried to match his movements, tried to give back to him, but he'd taken total control and all she could do was surrender to the ravaging passion.

By the time he lifted his head, her legs were trembling and she was clutching the front of his shirt just to keep herself upright.

He whispered, "I think we should go inside, don't you?"

Her lips felt swollen, prompting her to run the tip of her tongue over them at the same time she sucked in deep, ragged breaths. And though she should have taken the time to regain her senses and consider his loaded question, she didn't wait. She was tired of waiting.

"Yes," she murmured. "We should."

She followed him over to the door, which he quickly unlocked with a spare key hidden beneath a pot of cacti. Once they were inside, he switched on the nearest table lamp and beneath the dim glow Vanessa caught a brief glance of expensive, rustic-style furniture, a polished pine floor scattered with braided rugs and a wall of glass overlooking the deck. Beyond that, she saw nothing but Conall's dark face as he pulled her into his arms and began to kiss her all over again.

For long, long moments, they stood just inside the door, their bodies locked together, their lips clinging, tasting and searching for a closeness they couldn't quite attain. Unlike his ravaging kiss on the deck, this time his lips were slow and hot, luring her to a place where there was nothing but mindless pleasure.

The concept of time faded, along with their surroundings. When he finally ended the embrace and took her by the hand to lead her out of the room, she followed blindly and willingly down a narrow hallway with doors leading off both sides.

At the far end, they entered a bedroom with a wall of glass similar to the one they'd just left. Beyond it, the moon was a bright orb in the sky and its silver light illuminated the layout of the room, the king-sized bed and matching cedar armoire, a pair of stuffed armchairs by the window and a nightstand that could also be used as a desk.

Leading her toward the bed, Conall said, "This is the room I stay in whenever I'm up here. But that's not often."

"Why is that?" she asked huskily.

Their legs bumped into the side of the mattress and he quickly spun her into his arms. "Because you're not here," he said with a hungry growl.

She groaned with disbelief. "Oh, Conall."

He pulled her down onto the mattress and with the two of them lying face-to-face, he cupped a hand against her cheek. "It's true, Vanessa. Until you came to work for me, I think I'd forgotten about living. And I'd sure as hell forgotten about this."

With his arm around her waist, he urged her forward until the front of her body was pressed tightly to his. Vanessa's heart was pounding like a drumbeat deep in a hot jungle as his lips settled against her cheek, then slid open and wet to the side of her neck.

Desire bubbled within her before spreading like fingers of hot lava to every part of her body. Certain she was paralyzed by the incredible heat, she moaned and waited for a sense of normalcy to return to her limbs. It didn't. And in the back of her mind, she suddenly realized that everything about this and about Conall was different and new.

"I think… I might have forgotten, too," she whispered as his lips continued their heated foray against her throat. "Or maybe I never knew that it could feel like this."

Lifting his head, he gazed wondrously at her. "Vanna. Oh, baby."

It was all he said before his lips moved over hers and then his kiss was telling her how much he needed and wanted her. And for the moment that was enough for Vanessa. Words could come later.

Like a man wandering through a parched desert, Conall craved to drink from her lips, to bury himself in the moist folds of her body and restore the dry emptiness inside him. And though he was trying his best to control himself, to give her time to get used to being in his arms and to accept the idea of making love to him, the weeks, days, hours of wanting her had left him simmering far too long.

Before he could stop himself, he was tugging at her clothes, tossing them every which way until his hands and mouth had nothing but smooth skin beneath them. She felt like the petal of a flower and tasted even sweeter.

Without even knowing it, a groan rumbled deep in his throat as he explored her tight nipples, then on to the hollow of her belly, the bank of her hipbone and the tender slope of her inner thigh.

Above his head, he could hear her soft whimpers of need and the sound fueled him, thrilled him, empowered him in a way he'd never felt before. And when her fingers delved into his hair, her hips arched toward his searching mouth, he realized that without even trying she was giving him everything his body, his soul, had been craving for so long.

Desperate to have her, yet please her, he slipped his hand between her thighs, then his fingers into the very warm center of her. Her reaction was to suck in a harsh breath and then she released a guttural groan as his slow, tempting strokes caused her to writhe and beg for relief.

"Conall...please... I can't...wait!"

Her choked plea prompted him to pull his fingers away and quickly replace them with his tongue. As he lathed the moist folds, she began to pulsate and he supped at her pleasure, inhaled the unique scent of her until the ache in his loins threatened to overtake him.

While her body was still riding on a crested

wave, he moved up and over her, then sealing his lips over hers, he thrust deep inside her.

The intimate connection was so overwhelming it took his breath, and not until her legs wrapped around his waist and her hips arched toward him did he realize his body had gone stock-still. He used the moment to lift his head and gaze down at her face and for one split second he wished he'd looked elsewhere, anywhere but at the tenderness, the raw emotion radiating from her eyes. What he saw in the deep brown depths looked so much like love that he wanted to embrace it and run from it all at the same time.

Cupping a hand against her cheek, he tried to speak, to tell her with words exactly how much this moment meant to him. But nothing would form on his tongue except her name and it came out on a hoarse whisper.

"Vanna. My beautiful sweetheart."

Reaching up, she curled a hand around the back of his neck and pulled his face down to hers. "Make love to me, Conall."

Love. She wasn't labeling it as sex anymore. She was calling it love. And Conall couldn't argue the point. In spite of his effort to put a brake on his free-falling emotions, everything inside his heart was shouting that he loved this woman. And he could no more put a halt to his feelings than he could stop his body from moving against hers, from seeking the pleasure that only she could give him.

Chapter Ten

With her cheek resting against his damp chest, the sound of his rapid heartbeat merged with the blood rushing through her ears. Her hair was a damp tangle around her face while the rest of her body was covered with a fine sheen of sweat. Beyond Conall's shoulder she could see the glass wall, which was partially covered with dark drapes.

Sometime after they'd entered the bedroom, clouds had covered the moon and now bolts of lightning were streaking across the peaks of the distant mountains. The ominous threat of rain matched the turmoil going on inside of her and though she tried to push the dark feelings

away, tried to focus on the sheer wonder of
being in Conall's arms, she couldn't prevent a
wall of tears from stinging her eyes and thick-
ening her throat.

When his hand rested on her head and his
fingers began to push through her hair, she
did her best to speak. Talking would break the
spell, she told herself. Talking would make her
realize that what just happened between them
was normal and nothing out of the ordinary.
The earth hadn't shattered nor had her heart. It
was still beating in her chest and the world was
still turning on its axis. So why did she feel
as though everything had suddenly changed?

"It's going to rain," she said.

He murmured, "Not in here. We're dry and
cozy."

His hand left her hair to settle on her shoulder and Vanessa's eyelids drifted closed as his
fingers made lazy circles across her skin. She
wanted to stay in his arms forever. She wanted
to pretend that he loved her, that each time
he'd touched her, his heart had been guiding
him. But that would be fooling herself. And
she wasn't going to be a fool a second time
around. No matter how good he made her feel.

"It's getting late," she reminded him. "I have
to be going home soon."

His sigh ruffled the top of her hair. "It's already late. Being a little later isn't going to make much difference."

Tilting her head back, she looked at him. "Explaining this to Hannah is not going to be easy."

One side of his lips twisted upward. "Hannah isn't your mother. And why don't you simply tell her the truth? That you were out with me?"

She bit down on her bottom lip. "I don't know."

"Why? Are you ashamed of being here with me?"

"Not exactly."

His jaw thrust forward. "What is that supposed to mean?"

She swallowed as the raw thickness returned to her throat. "I guess what I'm trying to say is…that I'm feeling more sad than anything."

A puzzled frown puckered his forehead and then his expression quickly turned to one of concern. "Sad? Why, did I hurt you? Did I do something wrong and you're too embarrassed to tell me about it?"

A rush of pure love for him overcame her and she scooted her body upward until she could press her lips against his cheek. "Oh,

Conall, you did everything right. Perfect. I could make love to you over and over if...well, I suppose I'm just feeling sad because I know this is the end."

Next to hers, she could feel his body tense.

"End?" he asked inanely. "I thought it was just the beginning."

Easing out of his arms, she sat up on the side of the bed. Except for the intermittent flashes of lightning, the interior of the bedroom was completely black. She was glad the darkness was there to hide her tears.

"I can't keep being your secretary now, Conall. Not after this. It would never work."

The sheets rustled as he shifted toward her and then his hand was pushing the hair away from the back of her neck. As he pressed a kiss against her nape, he murmured, "I'm glad you said that, Vanessa. Like I said before, I don't want you to be my secretary. I want you to be my wife."

Groaning, she bent her head and squeezed her eyes against the burning tears. "Oh, Conall, please don't do this to me," she pleaded in a whisper. "Not tonight."

With his hands on her bare shoulders, he twisted her upper body toward him. "What am I doing to you that's so wrong, Vanna? I'm asking you to be my wife, to be at my side for the rest of our lives. A few minutes ago you said you could make love to me over and over. Did you mean that?"

"Yes. But marrying you—I can't. I can't live in a loveless marriage." She gestured toward the center of the bed. "Yes, the sex between us would be good—for a while. But after the initial luster wore off everything would feel empty...be empty. I want more than that."

His hand smoothed the hair back from her forehead and as her gaze flickered over his shadowed features, she suddenly felt as though she was looking at a different man. The soft and gentle expression in his eyes was something she'd never seen before and she didn't know what to think or expect.

"I want more than that, too, Vanna."

Wide-eyed, with her lips parted, she stared at him. "What are you saying?"

One corner of his mouth lifted. "You don't want to make any of this easy for me, do you?"

"Easy? Nothing about this is easy for me," she said flatly. "I've made too many mistakes, Conall. I don't want to keep making more."

A heavy breath slipped past his lips. "Neither do I," he admitted. "That's why...you have to know...that I love you."

Stunned, she shifted her body so that she was facing him directly. "Love? Who are you trying to kid? Me or yourself?" Angry and confused, she slipped off the bed and reached for her dress. "Either way, Conall, I'm not sure I can forgive you for this!"

Leaping off the bed, he snatched the dress from her hands before she could step into the garment. "What the hell are you talking about?" he demanded. "I'm trying to tell you how I feel about you—about us!"

"Sure. Sure you are." Since he'd confiscated her dress, she glanced around for something to cover her nakedness. Luckily his shirt was at her feet and she quickly jammed her arms into the sleeves and buttoned the front between her breasts. "What do you think I am? An idiot? A fool?"

Tossing her dress aside, he reached for her and though she wanted to resist, she couldn't. As soon as his hands wrapped around her shoulders, as soon as the front of his hard, warm body was pressed against hers, she was lost to him.

"Vanna," he began gently, "maybe I did pick the wrong time to confess my feelings. Maybe it does look all contrived to you. But I can't help that. I'm a rancher not some sort of

Romeo or playboy that knows exactly what to say or how to say it."

She wanted to believe him. Every beat of her heart was longing for his words to be true. But the scarred, wary side of her held back, refused to believe that this man could have changed. Especially for her.

"Maybe you're forgetting, Conall. You told me that you didn't believe in love. That it was a fairy-tale existence. Not a firm foundation for a marriage."

A mixture of regret and frustration twisted his features. "That was the bitterness in me doing the talking, Vanna. For a long time now I'd quit looking for a woman to love. I'd decided it wasn't worth the pain. But then you walked into my life and…oh, Vanna, believe me, I've tried not to love you. I've tried telling myself that you're just another woman, you're nothing special and I could do without you. But none of that has worked. I want you by my side. I need you in my bed, my life, in every way a man can need a woman. I love you. Pure and simple."

Even though she felt the safety barriers inside her begin to crumble, she tried her best to withstand his gentle persuasion. "And us just having sex had nothing to do with this sudden realization of yours," she said with skepticism.

His hands left her shoulders and began to roam against her back and farther down to the curve of her bottom. The familiar touch of his hands, even through the fabric of his shirt, was heating her flesh, reminding her body of the delicious pleasures he could give her.

"Would you call what just happened between us sex?" he countered. "You don't believe that. And neither do I. And as for realizing that I loved you—" dipping his head, he nuzzled his cheek against hers "—I think that happened a long time ago, Vanna. Even before that day you fainted in my arms. That's why I did my best to keep everything between us business. I didn't want to give myself the chance to let my feelings for you grow."

In spite of all the misgivings traipsing through her thoughts, Vanessa's heart began to beat with hope. Tilting her head back she gazed at him through shimmery eyes. "I didn't want to love you, either," she whispered, "but I do."

With a groan of relief, he captured her lips with his and with their mouths still locked, he lowered them both back onto the bed.

As he shoved his shirt off her shoulders

and began to nibble eagerly at one breast, she groaned in defeat. "Conall, the babies—"

"Are going to have me for a daddy," he murmured, his words muffled by her heated skin.

"But tonight—"

"You'll be getting home late. Very late."

More than a week later, Conall was standing beneath the shady overhang of a long shed row talking with Walt. In his early seventies with a face as wrinkled as a raisin, he was rawhide-tough and as dependable as the rise and fall of the sun. For longer than Conall had been alive, he'd been the man who made sure the barns, the stalls, the gallopers, the hot walkers, the grooms and everyone in between had what they needed to make their jobs easier and keep the horses in top-notch condition.

A stickler for making lists, Walt's hand-scribbled notes normally went to Liam's office first and then on to Conall's. But with Liam still out in California at the Del Mar track, he was making sure Conall was personally handed the written requests.

"Not asking for much this time, Mr. Conall," he said as Conall scanned the short piece of paper. "Mainly shavings and clippers. Had two pair of them burn up this week. They just ain't made to last like they used to be."

Even though it had been more than forty years since Walt had migrated over to New Mexico from South Texas, he still insisted on the mannerly form of putting the *Mr.* in front of Conall's name.

"Shavings, huh?" Conall mused out loud. "I just had a thousand yards of those delivered to the ranch last week. We already need more?"

"Yes, sir. That brother of yours has stalled nearly every two-year-old on this place and I think half of 'em needs to be turned to pasture. Save plenty of shavings like that. But you know Mr. Liam, he thinks they're all runners."

Conall grunted with amusement. "He's supposed to think like that, Walt. Otherwise, he might accidently turn a champion out to pasture."

The older man's grin was sly. "Well, we couldn't have that, could we?"

Giving Walt a companionable swat on the shoulder, Conall said, "It's time I got back to the office. Why don't you take the rest of the day off, Walt," he suggested. "You work too hard."

A scowl wrinkled Walt's features even more. "Look who's talkin'. Besides, I gotta help Travis repair the water trough in the yearling pen. Anything mechanical boggles that boy's mind. This younger generation is helpless. Slap-dab helpless."

Still muttering about Travis's incompetence, Walt turned and walked away. Conall headed in the opposite direction and was nearly at the end of the shed row when he spotted Brady, his younger brother, striding toward him.

Being a deputy for the Lincoln County sheriff's department kept Brady working random shifts, which didn't give Conall much opportunity to spend time with him. This evening Brady was still dressed in his uniform and Conall didn't have to ask if his day had been long. The man put in an extraordinary amount of hours on the job, yet even now there was a grin on his face, albeit a weary one.

If Conall was being totally honest with himself, he'd often been envious of his youngest brother. Brady had grown up to be the strong-minded, independent one of the Donovan boys. He'd chosen to go outside the family tradition of horse racing and take on a job that he quite obviously loved. Moreover, Brady had never experienced a moment's guilt over the decision. Whereas Conall had often felt bound, even restricted, by the duty of being the eldest son; the one that was meant to hold the Diamond D together for future generations.

"Hey, Conall," he greeted. "Are you heading toward the house or the office?"

As Brady took off the felt hat he was wearing and slapped it against his thigh to remove the dust, Conall gestured toward the part of the ranch yard where the office buildings were located.

"The office. And I'm glad you interrupted. I get damned tired of being cooped up."

Brady chuckled slyly. "With Vanessa? That's hard to believe."

Conall frowned. "Vanessa took the day off to go shopping with Maura. Mom's been sitting in for her, but she's already left me, too. One of these days I've got to take the time to hire an assistant to take over whenever Vanessa or Mom can't be around."

Clearly amused, Brady walked over to the nearest stall where a chestnut horse was poking his nose eagerly over the wooden gate that had him safely fastened inside the small square space. As he stroked Hot Charlie's nose, he said, "Mom probably hightailed it to the house 'cause you were too cranky to put up with."

Smiling, Conall walked over to join his

brother. "What are you talking about? I'm always Mr. Nice Guy."

"Well, maybe now that Vanessa has tamed you," he conceded. "You two set a wedding date yet?"

"Not yet. But we will soon."

"That's good." Brady glanced at him. "I haven't had a chance to tell you how glad I am that you're getting married again. I've been hoping for a long time that you'd find somebody special—like I found Lass."

Conall smiled ruefully. When Brady had first fallen in love with Lass, Conall had been worried sick about his younger brother and the whole situation he'd gotten himself into. At the time, Lass had been suffering from amnesia and hadn't known who she was or even if she had a home somewhere. Conall had been certain she was going to take Brady for a disastrous ride. He and Brady had even had cross words over the woman. But Conall would be the first to admit he'd been dead wrong about Lass. She'd made Brady a loving and devoted wife.

"Well, I didn't find her on the side of the road like you found Lass," Conall joked, "but she's definitely the right one for me."

Turning away from the horse, Brady gave

him a weary smile. "That's all that matters. When's Liam coming home?"

"I don't know. Probably not until Del Mar closes on Labor Day. So let's hope he's taking a liking to all that sun and surf."

Brady laughed out loud. "Liam in the surf? That'd be the day. He's spending every waking moment on the backside of the track. That's what he's doing." He slapped a hand over Conall's shoulder. "I've got to get going. Dallas is staying at Angel Wings an hour later tonight to accommodate a little girl who's just gotten over a long illness, so Lass is expecting me to drive over and fetch her before dinnertime. And since my wife and I haven't had dinner together in the past two weeks, she'll kill me if I'm late."

"I doubt it. Other than Vanna, I don't know of any woman who's more understanding than Lass."

Brady started to stride away, then at the last minute turned back toward Conall. "Oh. By the way, I came down here to tell you that we found out who crashed their vehicle through the fence—a teenage boy from over around Alto. The father found the damage to the truck and pressed his son for answers. The man is offering to pay for the fence repairs. I told him I'd discuss it with you and let him know."

Conall shook his head. "Money isn't the issue. I'd rather the boy do the labor to repair the fence. Teach him a hell of a lot better lesson than his dad bailing him out with money."

"That's exactly what I was thinking. I'll have a talk with the father and see what we can work out," Brady said, then grinned. "By the way, I hope Vanessa knows what a hell of a daddy those twins are getting."

Brady lifted his hand in farewell, then turned to hurry on to his waiting truck. Conall remained beside Hot Charlie's stall as all sorts of emotions swirled inside of him.

These past few days, he'd been torn between complete euphoria and stark terror. When Vanessa had made love to him and agreed to marry him, the joy he'd felt had put him on a cloud. She was everything he'd ever wanted in a woman and wife. Being with her, loving her, made his life complete. Yet in his quieter moments, nagging fear tried to intrude on his happiness.

There was going to be trouble—big trouble—if he didn't take Vanessa aside and talk to her about his condition. But since their night at the mountain cabin, when she'd agreed to

marry him, things had quickly begun to barrel
out of control. Not that he could use a hectic
routine as an excuse. If he'd been any sort of
man at all, he would have told her that night.
But at the time, he'd not had the courage or
the confidence to risk smashing the progress
he'd made with her. He'd felt…no, he'd *known*
that Vanessa needed more convincing of his
love and he needed more time to do that convincing.

But that had been more than a week ago and
now his mother and grandmother were already
planning an engagement party for the two of
them. In a matter of days, the ranch house
would be full of friends, family and acquaintances. Everyone would be expecting them to
announce their wedding date. But would there
even be a wedding, he wondered, once Vanessa discovered he was sterile?

Once he returned to the office there was a
stack of business calls he still needed to make.
But business would have to wait, he decided,
as he reached for the cell phone in his shirt
pocket. Talking to Vanessa couldn't. If she
was the wonderful, understanding woman that
he believed her to be, then she would accept
and empathize with the circumstance that had
never been his fault.

Buoyed by the thought, Conall punched in Vanessa's cell number. After the fourth ring he was expecting her voice mail to end the call when she suddenly answered.

"Hello, Conall," she said. "This is a surprise. I expected you to still be working."

"I am. Sort of. I've been down at the shed rows talking with Walt. But I'm on my way back to the office to make a few calls before I quit for the evening."

"Oh, do you need information? Maura and I are at the Blue Mesa having coffee. I can probably talk you through it."

He smiled to himself. No matter what the situation, Vanessa was always the consummate secretary. "Everything is okay here. I'm calling to see about us getting together tonight. I thought I'd drive over to your place. That way I could see the twins. And we could…talk."

Her low chuckle was sexy enough to curl his toes. "Talk? You really think that would happen?"

He closed his eyes as the images of her naked and writhing beneath him rolled into his mind. Talking to Vanessa tonight was going to be difficult. In more ways than one. "Well, we do have things to discuss. Important things. Like making a date for our wedding. And…

other things," he added. He drew in a deep breath and blew it out. "Will you be in town for much longer?"

"Not much, I don't think. Let me check with Maura," she told him. She went off the line, but in the background he could hear the faint sounds of music and the casual chatter of voices, intermingled with street traffic. When she finally returned, she said, "We'll be leaving here soon, Conall. So I'll be home by the time you get there."

"Great. I'll see you then, darlin'."

Vanessa closed her cell phone and reached for her cooling coffee. Across the outdoor table, Maura smiled shrewdly.

"So what's my brother doing? Already giving you orders before you even get married?"

Chuckling, Vanessa said, "He's my boss. He's supposed to give me orders."

With a good-natured groan, Maura shook her head. "It's clear that he has you right where he wants you."

After a long sip of coffee, Vanessa looked over the rim of her cup at her longtime friend. "I can truthfully say I'm right where I want to be."

Smiling with approval, Conall's eldest sister sliced her fork into a piece of blueberry pie.

"Hmm. Well, I can honestly say that Conall appears to be right where he wants to be, too." She chewed, swallowed, then released a sigh of contentment. "This is so nice, Vanessa, the two of us getting out like this together. Since you've returned to Lincoln County we've hardly had any time to spend together. I hope that changes and we can have more days like this. You've not even been out to see the Golden Spur yet."

"I will soon," Vanessa promised. "After we're married Conall wants to find someone to help me in the office. He thinks I need to be home with the twins for at least half of every workday and I agree with that. I want the twins to bond with me and know me as their mother, not just a woman they see in the mornings and at night. Still, I don't want to give up working completely. Does that sound selfish?"

"Not to me," Maura said between bites of the rich dessert. "After Riley was born I cut my weekly work hours down to half. And since Clancy arrived back in April I've cut them even more. But I've not quit nursing entirely. I believe some women need outside interest, too. Like me. Otherwise we'd become as dull as dishwater. And no man wants a dull wife."

Vanessa took a long sip of coffee before

she replied, "Well, working a half day will be plenty for me until the twins get older."

Maura smiled suggestively. "And who knows, by then you and Conall might want more children."

Vanessa felt a blush creep across her cheeks. If she'd not had the forethought to stay on the oral birth control she'd used during her marriage, she would probably be pregnant with Conall's child at this moment. That night they'd first made love, she'd been so besotted and lost in the man she'd forgotten to mention she was protected and apparently he'd forgotten to ask. Later, when she tried to assure him that there was nothing to worry about, that she was on oral contraceptives, he'd quickly dismissed the whole thing. As though getting her pregnant would be a welcome idea with him.

She'd not yet talked with him about having any future children. But she had no doubts that he would want them. As crazy as he was about the twins, she couldn't imagine him wanting to stop with just the two.

"Maybe," Vanessa said, then before she could stop it, a happy laugh slipped past her lips. "Oh, Maura, it's still hard for me to take everything in. First the twins and now becoming Conall's wife. In my wildest imaginings I couldn't have pictured this happening to me. I look back now and wonder why I was fighting Conall so hard and refusing to accept his proposal."

Her pie gone, Maura pushed the plate aside and reached for her coffee. "I remember the feeling well. I fought Quint for a long time before I ever agreed to marry him. But a woman wants to know she's loved for herself, not because of a baby. And Gilbert had done such a job of deceiving me that I...was scared to trust any man. Thank God Quint was persistent."

"I'm very happy that Conall didn't give up on me, either."

Vanessa placed her empty cup back on its saucer and reached for her handbag. "If you're ready we should probably be going. I need to tidy up the house—and myself—before Conall gets there."

Reaching across the table, Maura placed her hand over Vanessa's. "Before we go, I just wanted to say how glad I am that you're going to be my sister-in-law. I couldn't have picked any better woman for my brother. He's been so...well, dark and lost after the mess he went through with Nancy. I was afraid he'd never let himself love again. But you've made him so happy and I know you always will. You'd never try to hurt or manipulate him like she did. And you'd certainly never stop loving him just because of his condition."

Vanessa suddenly froze. "Condition?" she repeated blankly.

Maura's auburn brows pulled together. "Why, yes. You know—*his condition.*"

Thrown for a loop, Vanessa's mind began to race down a tangle of dark roads. If there was something personal about Conall that she wasn't aware of, something he should have told her already, the last thing she wanted was for Maura to explain. That could only cause trouble between brother and sister. And whatever it was, she wanted to hear it directly from the man she planned to marry.

"Oh, yes," she said with feigned dawning. "That… None of that matters to me."

Maura's smile was full of approval and relief. "That's one of the reasons I've always loved you, Vanessa. You don't expect a person to be perfect."

Her mouth suddenly felt like she'd walked through Death Valley in mid-July. She reached for her water glass and after a long drink, tried to speak casually. "I'm hardly perfect myself, Maura. I can't expect others to be."

Just as Maura started to reply, her cell phone

went off and the other woman quickly began to fish the device from her handbag. Vanessa was grateful for the diversion. She couldn't continue to fake this train of conversation.

"Excuse me, Vanessa, it's Quint. I'd better see what he needs."

While Maura exchanged a few short words with her husband, Vanessa's mind tumbled end over end. What could be wrong with Conall? A recurring health problem? That was hard to believe. During the time she'd worked for him, she'd never seen him sick or even close to it. He appeared as healthy as the horses he bred and raised.

The snapping sound of Maura's phone being shut jerked Vanessa out of her whirling thoughts and she looked across the table at her friend's apologetic face.

"I hate to end the day so abruptly, Vanna, but Quint's grandfather is feeling a bit puny and he wants me to drive out to Apache Wells and check on him before I go home. It's forty minutes from here, so I need to hit the road."

As she stood up, she tossed several bills onto the table. "That ought to take care of everything here."

Rising to her feet also, Vanessa quickly

grabbed up the money and thrust it back at the other woman. "Here. I'll take care of things."

"No arguments. It's my treat today, sweetie." She pressed a quick kiss on Vanessa's cheek. "See you soon. And I promise you that Conall's eyes are going to pop out of his head when he sees you in the dress we found today."

Smiling as brightly as she could, Vanessa waved her friend off, then went to pay the check. A few minutes later, she was on the highway, driving home to Tinnie as fast as the speed limit would allow.

Conall had never been known for being a nervous person. In fact, his brothers had often accused him of having ice water in his veins and his mother had regularly referred to him as a piece of unmoving granite. But if they could see his insides now as he drove to Vanessa's place, they would all believe they were looking at some other man, not him. His stomach was clenched into a tight, burning knot and his heart was hammering at such a rate, the blood was pounding like a jackhammer against his temples.

He'd never agonized over discussing anything with anyone. Especially when he knew he'd be talking to a level-headed, sensible person. And Vanessa was definitely both of those things. Plus, she was understanding. So he had nothing to worry about, he told himself as he pulled his truck to a stop in front of the small Valdez house. Except his whole future.

Chapter Eleven

Vanessa answered the door after his first knock and before he stepped over the threshold, he pulled her into his arms and placed a long, reckless kiss on her lips.

"Mmm," she exclaimed with a little laugh. "Gauging by that greeting I'd say you've missed me a little today. Maybe it's a good thing I told Hannah she could have the evening off."

His arms tightened briefly around her waist and as the sweet scent of her rose to his nostrils, he desperately wished the only thing he needed to say to her were words of love and longing.

He peered over her shoulder. "She's not here?"

Vanessa stepped back and allowed him to enter the house. As she shut the door behind him, she said, "No. She left a half hour ago. I've been feeding the twins and now they're both down for the count."

"Oh. I was hoping they'd still be awake," he said as they gravitated away from the door, to the middle of the small living room. "It seems like ages since I've had a chance to hold them."

"It seems like ages since you've held me," she replied.

With an eager groan he pulled her into his arms and kissed her again, but this time he sensed she wasn't fully focused on him and when he lifted his head, he could see there was a tiny frown creasing her smooth forehead.

"What's wrong?"

"Nothing. I hope." Turning away from him, she gestured toward the kitchen. "Would you like something to eat?"

"No. Maybe later."

She clasped her hands in front of her. "All right. You said you wanted to talk. Let's talk."

For some reason he couldn't figure, she was on edge, even a tad cool, and he realized her unusual mood was only going to make his task harder.

"I'm trying to decide if we should discuss anything right now." Rather than make his way toward the couch, he continued to search her face. The closer inspection revealed a paleness he'd not noticed when she'd first answered the door. "You're not yourself tonight."

Her shoulders suddenly sagged and she let out a long breath. "Okay, I confess. I'm not myself. I'm actually worried sick about you."

Conall frowned with amused confusion. "Me? I'm great. Everything about me is great. And it'll be even better after we set our wedding date."

With a look of enormous relief, she sagged limply toward him and rested her cheek against the middle of his chest. "Oh, thank God. I thought...well, I've been imagining all sorts of horrible things."

Totally confused, Conall wrapped his arms tightly around her. "Why would you be doing that, honey? Surely you can see that everything is fine with me."

"I know," she said with a tiny sniff. "But I was afraid that...well, after what Maura said, that you might have a recurring disease or something. Since she's a nurse and—"

For once Conall felt as though there was actually ice water in his veins and it was freezing him with dread. "What exactly did Maura say?" he asked stiffly.

Leaning back, she looked up at him. "Nothing particular. Just something offhand about your condition. I didn't press her to explain. Whatever it is, I wanted to hear it from you."

With a sinking feeling in the pit of his stomach, he took her by the arm and led her over to the couch. "I think we'd both better sit," he said.

By the time they were settled and facing each other on the cushions, her brown eyes were dark with concern. Conall reached for one of her hands and clasped it tightly between the two of his.

"What is it, Conall? The way you're looking at me—it frightens me."

"I'm sorry. I didn't mean to." He shook his head, then lifted his face toward the ceiling and closed his eyes. "I'm not doing this right. But then, I don't guess there is a right way," he murmured. "I should have told you about this days ago. Weeks ago, even. But I couldn't bring myself to."

"Why?"

Struggling to keep the bitterness from his

voice, he said, "Because the information has always produced a negative reaction. Especially with women."

Her brows arched with surprise. "Women? I don't understand. You're certainly not frigid or impotent."

If he hadn't felt so sick inside he could have laughed. "No. I'm glad you figured that out."

Her free hand moved over his and squeezed tightly. "I don't know what this is about. But there's nothing you could tell me that would make me stop loving you, Conall."

"I hope to God that's true, Vanessa. I hope a few days from now we'll remember this moment and smile."

Her lips gently curved at the corners. "Being with you anytime makes me smile," she said, then laughed softly. "I sound like a hopeless cornball, don't I?"

Leaning forward, he pressed a kiss against her forehead. "And I've never seen a more lovely cornball."

She sighed. "Oh, Conall, even if you are ill I can deal with it. We'll deal with it together."

Easing his hand from beneath hers, he touched the side of her face. "I'm not ill, Vanessa, I promise. But I was once. When I was a very young child just learning to walk I had a viral infection that caused me to have a very high fever. I ended up having convulsions and my parents feared for my life. But eventually my body fought off the infection and I got well without any lasting effects, it seemed."

Her head swung back and forth. "Why are you telling me this now, Conall? I don't understand."

His eyes caught hers as he forced the words off his tongue. "Because you need to know why—why I can't have children."

She stared and he could see from the confusion crossing her face that she was having difficulty absorbing what he'd just said.

"Do you mean…you—"

"I'm sterile, Vanessa. The fever affected my reproductive system. It doesn't occur often, but it does happen from time to time. And I didn't even know that anything was wrong until Nancy and I tried to get pregnant."

"Oh. Oh, Conall…this is—" Her whole body sagged as though the air had literally been knocked from her. "I wasn't expecting anything like this."

Slowly, she pulled her hand from his and rose to her feet. Conall stayed on the couch and watched as she began to absently move about the small room. Eventually she stopped at a small end table and picked up a framed photo of her parents. There was raw pain on her face as she studied the image and in that moment Conall hated himself. If he'd not fallen in love with her, if he'd not pushed her to marry him, she would have eventually found someone else, someone who could give her everything. Now, God only knew what all this was doing to her.

"I'm sorry, Vanessa," he said hoarsely.

She didn't respond and after a moment he rose to his feet and walked across the room. As he came to stand beside her, she placed the photograph back on the table, then turned to face him.

"I'm sorry, too, Conall, that such a terrible thing ever happened to you. But mostly I'm sorry that you felt you couldn't tell me—long before—before I fell in love with you!"

Tears began to stream down her face and he realized there was an ache in the middle of his chest that made it almost impossible to breathe. If he was having a heart attack he probably deserved it, he thought. But he wasn't ready to die. No, there was so much that he wanted for the two of them and the twins.

"You're right. I should have. But...you weren't exactly warming up to the idea of having any sort of relationship with me. If I'd suddenly blurted out the fact that I was sterile, you would have turned your back on me and not given us any chance for a future together."

Her mouth fell open. "How do you know that I would have reacted that way? You didn't try!"

He curled his hands over the top of her shoulders. "Would you have given us a chance, Vanessa? Answer me truthfully."

Her tear-filled eyes were full of agony as she searched his face. "I don't know. I've always wanted children. Jeff wouldn't give me any and—"

"You have two children now," he pointed out. "Two beautiful, wonderful children. I want to be a father. Just like you want to be a mother."

A perceptive light suddenly flickered in her eyes. "Ahh. I wasn't thinking. But I am now," she said stiffly. "You want to be a father and I have two babies." She rapped her fist against the side of her head. "What a fool I've been! That's what this has been about all along. Everything you've done and said was all for the babies! I was just a...side dish for you!"

His face felt like a stiff clay mask as he spoke in a low, purposeful tone. "I thought... I hoped and prayed that you would be different from the others. That's one of the reasons why I fell in love with you. Because deep down I believed you would accept me for the man that I am instead of persecuting me for what I can't be. I can see now that I was wrong. Again," he added bitterly.

Her expression incredulous, she shook her head. "Don't try to make me the culprit, Conall! You asked me to marry you because of the twins!"

In spite of the pain ripping through him, the corners of Conall's mouth tilted into a wan smile. "You finally got something right about this whole situation, Vanessa. The twins were the very reason I proposed to you. I like to think they need me just as much as I need them. But mainly I figured you having the twins would make my sterility easier for you to accept. You already had two children and I was hoping they and me would be enough for you. I can clearly see we're not."

Not bothering to wait for any sort of reply she might give him, he snatched up his hat, levered it onto his head and quietly let himself out of the house.

The next morning, after a night that had passed like a wide-awake nightmare for Vanessa, she dragged herself out of bed before daylight, and chugged down a cup of coffee before she finally found the courage to reach for the phone.

As she'd hoped, Conall wasn't yet in the office and she felt a measure of guilt when the voice mail answered. But she was in such a raw, emotional state she knew the mere sound of his voice would break her into sobs. Talking directly to him would only make matters worse.

Her throat aching, she swallowed and forced herself to speak. "This is Vanessa. I'm calling to let you know I won't be in to work today. If you…feel you need to replace me permanently I'll understand. Goodbye."

As soon as she snapped the phone shut she began to weep and when Hannah walked into the kitchen, tears were still seeping from Vanessa's eyes.

On the way to the coffeepot, the woman yawned and swiped a tangle of dark hair from her face. "My, you're up early," she exclaimed. "Do you have to go into work earlier than usual this morning?"

Vanessa hurriedly made an effort to wipe her eyes. "No, I'm not going in today. I—I'm not sure I'll be working for...the Diamond D anymore."

Pausing as she reached for a mug, Hannah glanced over her shoulder and suddenly noticed Vanessa's tearstained face. "What in the world is going on?"

Swallowing hard, Vanessa answered in a hoarse voice. "I don't know where to begin, Hannah. Everything is...over."

Forgetting the coffee, the woman hurried over to where Vanessa sat at the small dining table and curled an arm around her shoulders. "Are you ill? I'll get the babies ready and drive you in to town to see a doctor."

Since Hannah had become the twins' nanny, the two women had grown to be fast friends and Vanessa was beginning to think of her more as a sister than anything. At this very moment she felt like falling into Hannah's arms and sobbing her eyes out.

"No. I—I'm not ill." She looked away from the other woman and struggled to gather her composure. "Something happened last night— between me and Conall. I— We're not going to be getting married...like we'd planned."

Stepping back, Hannah looked at her. "Oh, no! I'm not going to believe this, honey. You two—why, you're perfect for each other."

Closing her eyes, Vanessa pressed her fingertips against her burning eyelids. Last night when Conall had walked out the door, she'd felt her heart rip right down the middle and for a few moments, she'd almost run after him. She'd wanted him to understand just how wrong he was about her. It wasn't his sterility that was a problem with her. It was the fact that being a father to the twins appeared to be far more important to him than being a husband to her.

But she'd not run after him. Pride, confusion and anger had all stopped her. Now, as the morning sun was beginning to creep across the kitchen floor, she wondered if she'd saved herself from another loveless marriage, or ruined the best thing that could have ever happened to her.

Sighing, she said, "Nothing is perfect in this world, Hannah."

"It's clear you're not thinking straight this morning, Vanessa. And I'm not going to pry into what happened. I'm just going to tell you to give yourself time. Whatever happened between the two of you will work itself out. I just know it."

Vanessa wished she had the other woman's optimism, but at the moment all she could see was a long bleak road ahead of her. Even if she'd misjudged Conall's motives for marrying her, she'd hurt him deeply with all her accusations. She seriously doubted he would ever want anything else to do with her.

"I seriously doubt it, Hannah. And I...well, I hate to bring it up, but if Conall fires me then I won't be able to keep you on as the twins' nanny." The idea of losing both Conall and Hannah brought a fresh spurt of tears to her eyes. "I'm so sorry."

Squeezing Vanessa's shoulder, she said, "Look, honey, quit borrowing trouble. Conall is the one who hired me for this job and he's the one who signs my checks. Until he tells me otherwise, I'll be here. Now put your chin up and help me fix us a bit of breakfast before the twins start yelling for theirs."

Almost two weeks later, Vanessa was surprised by a call from Gold Aspen Manor. The doctor had pronounced Alonzo fit enough to leave the nursing home for a few hours and she'd wasted no time in fetching him away from the facility and bringing him to the only home he'd known for the past sixty years.

Playing with the twins had left a sparkle in his eyes and now that they'd fallen asleep, her father was exploring the backyard, the patch where he'd grown vegetables and the acre-sized pen that held his beloved goats. At the moment, one of the nannies had trotted up to him and Vanessa's eyes misted over as she watched him stroke the goat's head.

Having her father home again, even for a few short hours, was the only bright thing that had happened since her break with Conall.

Break. Was that the right word for it? she wondered bleakly. It felt more like a dead-end crash to her.

With a heavy sigh, she turned her gaze to the pot of white daisies sitting in the middle of the patio table. *He loves me. He loves me not.* Plucking the petals couldn't tell her, Vanessa thought sadly. And as for Conall, he'd not even bothered to try.

Since the morning she'd called and left a message, she'd only talked to him once and that was when he'd called her later that same day. He'd been cool and brusque as he'd informed her that he'd gotten her message and that she needn't worry about coming in to work today or any day—he could handle things without her. She'd tried to get in a reply, to explain that she needed time to think things through, but he'd not given her a chance to say anything. Instead, he'd quickly ended the call with a cool goodbye and she'd not seen or heard from him since.

Had she really expected to hear from him? she miserably asked herself. Perhaps. Deep down she'd hoped and prayed that she'd been wrong about him, about his motives, about all the harsh things she'd accused him of. But he'd not made any effort to prove her wrong. And she couldn't humble herself to ask him to.

I believed you would accept me for the man that I am instead of persecuting me for what I can't be.

For the past couple of weeks Conall's low voice had sounded over and over in her head. His words continued to haunt and confuse her. Was she blaming him, punishing him for simply being unable to have children? No. She wasn't that sort of woman. She was using common sense. She was simply refusing to jump into another loveless marriage.

The feel of her father's warm hand on her shoulder had her looking up and she did her best to smile at him. "The goats are happy to see you," she said.

"They're fat. You've been feeding them good." He eased onto the chair opposite his daughter while glancing over to a shaded part of the patio where the twins were sleeping in a portable playpen. "The babies are growing fast. They'll soon walk."

Vanessa's gaze followed her father's and as she watched the sleeping babies, her heart swelled with a mixture of emotions. Even if she'd given birth to the twins herself, she couldn't love them any more. They were her children to raise and nourish, to teach and guide, to love and cherish. No matter how a child came in to a person's life, it was a precious gift and she'd been given not one, but two gifts.

Now, each time she looked at Rose and Rick, she thought of Conall. Unless he married a woman who already had children, or adopted some of his own, he would never know the joys of being a father. It wasn't right or fair and her heart ached for his loss. But the ache didn't stop there. Missing him, wanting and needing him, filled her with such pain she doubted she would ever recover.

Pulling her thoughts back to her father's remark, she said, "Yes, in a few months they'll be walking and I'll be chasing after them."

Even though Conall hadn't formally fired her, when he'd told her goodbye over the phone there'd been finality in his voice. He'd obviously decided she couldn't bring herself to work for him. And he clearly wasn't going to ask her to return to her job. As for Hannah, the woman had stuck to her guns. Unless Conall terminated her position, she insisted on staying with Vanessa and the babies. And so far, he'd not told Hannah that her job as the twins' nanny was finished.

Vanessa didn't know what to think about the situation. Did he love the twins that much?

"What are you going to do about a job?"

Caught off guard by Alonzo's remark, she looked across the table to see he was studying her closely. It was almost like her father had been reading her thoughts. But then, she'd never been able to keep anything from either of her parents. She was as transparent as a piece of cellophane tape, until it came to Conall. He'd been unable to see how much she loved him, how much she wanted his love in return.

"What do you mean?"

He grimaced. "I know about your job at the Diamond D, my daughter. And your fight with Conall."

Vanessa drew in a sharp breath. Since she'd picked up her father earlier in the day, he'd not mentioned anything about Conall or even asked why she wasn't working today. Vanessa had been putting off telling her father that she'd quit her job and her relationship with Conall. She'd known it would upset him and she'd been trying to think of some way to approach the subject without making it sound like her life was in a mess.

But it was in a mess. And avoiding the issue wasn't going to make her or her father feel any better about it, she decided.

"Who told you?"

"Conall. He came last week to see me. And explain." Alonzo shook his grizzled head. "I'm not happy, Vanessa. You're wrong. Wrong."

Sighing heavily, Vanessa looked away from her father's penetrating gaze. "I'm sorry I've disappointed you, Dad. But things…just didn't work out for us. That's all. I'm moving on. He's moving on. I'll get another job soon. In fact, Eric has already offered me a job at the Billy the Kid and I'll probably take it. So everything will be okay."

"Will it?"

Her lips pressed together, she rose from the chair and walked over to the playpen. Rick was beginning to stir, so she reached down and picked up her son. The warm weight of the baby cradled against her breasts was momentarily reassuring.

"Why not?" Vanessa countered his question with one of her own. "I've been supporting myself for years now. Jeff rarely lifted a hand to help me make ends meet. I'm not worried."

Alonzo spit out several curse words, further proof that his speech and his health was rapidly returning.

"What is this? You talk about money? Money is nothing. Nothing."

With Rick snuggled in her arms, she walked back over to her father. "It's something when you don't have it." She cast him a censuring glance. "Isn't that why you wanted me to marry Conall? So that I'd be financially secure?"

More curse words slipped past his lips and Vanessa shook her head. "It's a good thing the twins aren't old enough to hear you, otherwise I'd have to cover their ears."

"Hearing me cuss—you think that's bad?" He snorted. "Not near as bad as you explaining to them why Conall won't be their daddy."

Vanessa sat back down and positioned her son against her shoulder. As she patted Rick's back, she asked, "Just why do you think I'm not…marrying Conall?"

"Because he can't give you any more babies. The twins aren't enough for you, I guess."

Vanessa had thought she couldn't hurt any more than she had these past two weeks, but she was wrong. Her father's impression of her had always been important to her. Ever since she was a tiny girl, she'd wanted him to admire her, be proud of her. When she disappointed him it cut something deep inside her.

Trying to swallow away the tears burning her throat, she said, "You have this all wrong, Dad. I'm not not marrying Conall because he's sterile! Even if I didn't have the twins, that wouldn't matter to me. It's because he doesn't love me—he was using me to become a father. That's all!"

Alonzo sadly shook his head at her. "I hope to God your mama is not hearing you. Tears would be in her eyes."

"I guess as a daughter I've been a disappointment to you both," Vanessa said flatly. "But can't you see, Dad? I made a bad mistake with Jeff. I don't want to repeat it with Conall. I—" Her eyes pleaded with him to understand. "I just can't go through that sort of pain again."

"You think Conall only wanted the twins? I thought you were smarter than that, my daughter. Conall isn't ugly or stupid or poor. There're plenty of single women around that need a daddy for their children. You aren't the only one. Wonder why he isn't proposing marriage to them?"

"Probably because he hasn't gotten off the ranch to meet any of them yet," Vanessa retorted.

Alonzo snorted. "And what about all those orphanages with babies that need a home? If all he wanted was to be a daddy, he could do that without you. He asked you to marry him because he loves you. But you can't see that. All you can see is Jeff. You're still hung up on that sorry excuse for a man."

Outraged, Vanessa shot straight to her feet. "That is not true! I love Conall! You know that!"

Nodding, Alonzo said, "I know it. But does Conall? Maybe you should be telling him instead of me."

Vanessa sank weakly back into the chair. Her father was making sense, a lot more sense than she'd made this past couple of weeks. Which made her feel even more like a fool. But what could she do about it now? Conall appeared to have already washed his hands of her. "I'm not sure he'd want to hear it," she mumbled uncertainly.

For the first time since he'd sat down at the table, Alonzo smiled. "It'd be worth a try."

Easing Rick from her shoulder, she cradled the baby against her breasts and as she gazed down at her son's tiny face, she knew she had to see Conall, she had to convince him that she loved him for the man he was and nothing else mattered.

Chapter Twelve

The next morning, shortly after daylight, Conall broke from the normal routine of reading his messages and walked the quarter-mile distance to the training track. Now, as he stood next to his father at the pipe railing, he tried to focus his attention on one of the ranch's most promising runners.

Like a gull skimming the ocean, the dark brown filly was moving smoothly over the track, floating as though she had wings on her hooves. Her neck was level and outstretched, her ears perked with reserve energy. On the last turn, she lay close to the rail and then sprinted down the homestretch.

"Look at that!" Doyle practically shouted. "Juan didn't even have to ask her to change leads!" His father punched the button on the stopwatch before turning to look at Conall. "Kate's Kitten is going to be a queen, boy! She's not only fast, she's smart. When was the last time we got a combination like that?"

"When Red Garland was born," Conall was quick to answer.

Doyle stared at him with surprise and then he chuckled. "You got me there. But Kate's Kitten is right behind her. We're going to have two queens on our hands."

A wan smile touched Conall's lips. Even though the sight of the galloping filly had been beautiful, he couldn't work up near the enthusiasm that his father was displaying. But then, there wasn't much of anything that could lift his spirits these days. Not since he'd walked out of Vanessa's house. He'd not looked back that day. But he'd not needed to look back to see that he'd left his heart in her hands.

Everything you've done and said was all for the babies! I was just a...side dish for you!

Even now, after nearly two weeks had passed, the accusation that Vanessa had flung at him still had the power to hurt. Unlike an aching tooth that could be pulled out and thrown away, the words continued to claw at him and he didn't know what to do to dull the pain, much less make it go away.

"Liam will be thrilled to hear you say that about Kate's Kitten," Conall remarked. "And Grandmother will be happy to hear that her namesake has yet to disappoint."

Doyle frowned at his eldest son. "Hell, Conall, *you're* supposed to be thrilled, too. Instead you look like you did when you were a kid and I just ordered you to your bedroom to study for exams."

Conall held back a weary groan. With Vanessa no longer sitting at her desk, nothing seemed the same, felt the same. He'd walked down here to the track this morning in hopes of giving his mind a short reprieve of her image, of the tortured thoughts he couldn't cast away. But so far he'd not felt one moment of relief.

"Sorry, Dad. I am excited about Kate's Kitten. It's just that… I've had a lot of things on my mind here lately."

Doyle stuffed the stopwatch in his shirt pocket as Conall absently watched the jockey jump to the ground and hand the filly's reins to the waiting hot walker.

"Guess it doesn't have anything to do with that little secretary of yours."

Conall grimaced. "She was more than my secretary, Dad. She was the woman I was planning to marry. Now she...well, she's not even my secretary anymore."

The tall dark-haired man's expression turned to one of concern as he eyed his son. "Hell, Conall, we all knew you were planning to marry Vanessa and we all know those plans went awry. But no one has mentioned anything to me about Vanessa quitting her job."

Conall's gaze dropped to the toes of his boots. "I haven't exactly told anyone that Vanessa has quit. Since Mom is filling in at the office, I just explained to her that Vanessa was taking some time off, that's all."

"Instead, Vanessa quit. Is that it? Because you two can't see eye-to-eye on your romance." Squinting at a far off group of horse barns, he said in a gentler voice, "Well, that's not surprising. When a woman gets angry she doesn't want a man getting too close. If he does get near, she'll raise her hackles and hiss. I can see where she wouldn't want to be cooped up in an office with you."

Conall wiped a hand over his face. He couldn't remember the last time he'd slept the night through and his lack of rest was only compounding the mental agony he was going through. "She accused me of wanting to marry her just for the twins."

Doyle sighed. "In case you didn't know, your sister Maura is heartsick. She thinks she's the cause of all of this."

Shaking his head, Conall turned his gaze back on the exercise track. At the moment a chestnut colt was being trotted around the mile oval, but Conall wasn't really seeing the beautiful Thoroughbred, he was seeing Vanessa's face, the way she'd looked when he'd told her that he couldn't have children. It was like he'd punched her in the stomach.

A grimace tightened his weary features. "Maura isn't to blame for anything. I wasn't planning to marry Vanessa without telling her about my condition. Maybe I should have done it sooner, but I kept thinking our relationship needed to be more solid before I sprung something like that on her. Apparently there wasn't anything solid about it," he added bitterly.

Stepping closer, Doyle rested a comforting hand on Conall's shoulder. "You think she turned her back on you because you can't give her children, don't you?"

Filled with agony, he looked at his father. "Oh, God, Dad, what hurts the most is that I really thought she was different. That she would accept me just the way I am. I don't want to believe that she's like Nancy or the others that backed away from me like I was a ruined man."

"Conall, just because I'm your father doesn't make me an expert on women. God knows I've only loved one all of my life and she's more than enough to keep me confused. But from the little time I've been around her, Vanessa seems like a very sensible woman."

Conall grunted. "What does that make me, an idiot?"

"Sort of."

"Thanks, Dad," Conall said with sarcasm. "That really makes me feel better."

"Hell, son, I'm not trying to make you feel better. I'm trying to help you fix things. Forget about Nancy and what came about with her. Forget about the other women that turned tail and ran. Nothing is going to be fixed with you and Vanessa until you first start accepting yourself. You need to realize that siring a child doesn't necessarily make a man a man or a father a father. You're much a man in my eyes, son. And I think you are in Vanessa's, too. Don't give up on her."

Doyle gave him one final pat on the back, then strode off in the direction of Kate's Kitten and the hot walker. Watching him go, Conall continued to lean against the white railing as his father's words reverberated in his head.

Had he been too hard on himself all these years? God knows, he'd tried hard to live up to the role of being the eldest Donovan son. He'd tried his best to always be the strong one, the one who rarely, if ever, failed, the one who would leave an admirable pattern for his younger brothers to follow.

When he'd learned of his inability to have children, he'd felt like a total failure, like he'd let his family down in the worst kind of way. But in the tradition of his role, he'd glued on his iron-man image and pretended to his family and acquaintances that he was tough enough to swallow anything life handed him.

Scrubbing his face with one hand, he turned away from the track and lifted his gaze toward the far mountain range where Vanessa's little house sat near a shrubby arroyo. It was no wonder, he thought, that Vanessa had struggled to believe that he truly loved her. For most of his adult life he'd been pretending, making an art out of hiding his feelings.

If he ever hoped to have another chance with her, he was going to have to go to her, open himself wide and hope that she could see what was truly inside of him.

His strides long and purposeful, he hurried back toward the office. If his mother had arrived to fill in at Vanessa's desk, he would send her home and reroute all his calls to the ranch's general office, he decided. If he hurried, he could drive over to Vanessa's house in twenty minutes.

His thoughts were so caught up in his plans that when he arrived back at the block of offices, he didn't notice the car parked next to his Ford truck at the side of the building. When he stepped inside, he glanced over, expecting to see his mother. Instead, Vanessa was sitting at the desk, sifting through a stack of correspondence as though she'd never been gone.

"Vanna!"

He didn't know whether he'd shouted her name or whispered it. All he knew was that she looked like a beautiful dream come true and his boots couldn't carry him across the room fast enough.

She looked up as he approached her desk and as their gazes met, her lips parted and he could see the movement of her throat as she swallowed.

"Hello, Conall."

"Where is Mom?"

She tried to smile and he was amazed to see that she was pale and nervous. Didn't she realize that she was holding all the cards, his very heart in her hands?

"When Fiona found me here, she went back home." She placed the papers she'd been holding back on the desktop and then with her eyes still on his face, folded her hands together in a tight steeple. "Since you never formally fired me I was hoping you needed your secretary back."

Amazed and shocked, he stared at her while his heart began to bump and thump with hope. "Did you honestly think I wouldn't want you here?"

Her head jerked back and forth. "I...didn't know. You walked out and—"

"That was a stupid stunt on my part."

Her eyes wide and hopeful, she rose to her feet. "You were hurt," she said in a raw whisper. "And I should have never said those awful things to you."

Fast as lightning, he streaked around the desk and tugged her into his arms. "Vanna! Oh, God, I'm so sorry. I've done everything wrong and—"

She placed a shushing finger against his

lips. "So have I. Maybe we both have. But that doesn't matter now. Does it?"

For an answer, his lips swooped down on hers. The sweet, familiar taste of her kiss was a soothing balm to his battered heart and it was a long, long time before he ever lifted his head.

"My darling, I...when I stepped through the door a few moments ago I was about to tell Mom to forget about working today. I'd already planned to drive over to see you—to see if you'd be willing to listen to me."

"Listen? You don't need to explain anything, Conall. I—"

Before she could finish, he grabbed her by the hand and led her into his office. After shutting the door behind them, he urged her over to the couch. After they were sitting, their knees together, hands clasped tightly, he said, "I need to explain a lot of things, Vanessa. I need to say them as much as you need to hear them."

Nodding, she said, "All right. But first, I just want to say... I love you. That I never stopped loving you."

His heart was so full he thought it would burst; he lifted a hand and reverently touched her cheek. "Vanessa, I was wrong in not telling you about my condition long before anything started to develop between us. But I guess it was something—well, I was trying to convince myself that with you it wouldn't matter."

Through a mist of watery tears, she smiled at him. "It doesn't matter if we can't have more children the conventional way," she assured him. "I don't care about that. I didn't care the day you told me about it. I wanted to be the reason you wanted to marry me. Not the twins. That's all. And I was quick to jump to the wrong conclusion. Because I guess I never believed I was good enough to deserve your love. I never could totally believe that you wanted me, needed me in that way."

Amazed by her confession, he shook his head. "Oh, Vanna, that's awful. How could you think such a thing? You're the most precious woman I've ever known."

Bending her head, she murmured, "Jeff squashed my ego, Conall. He never saw me as a wife that he loved and cherished. He saw me as a workhorse, a provider for him. And I could only think that you saw me as a way to have children—not as a wife."

Sighing, he pushed his fingers gently into the rich brown hair at her temple. "And I thought you couldn't love me because I was sterile." His mouth twisting to a wry slant, he went on. "You see, when Nancy and I married,

I had no idea that I was unable to father children. When we started trying to get pregnant and nothing happened, we both went through a battery of health tests. The minute the doctor gave us the news, something twisted inside of her, warped her into someone that I hardly recognized."

Lifting her head, Vanessa searched his face. "Didn't she stop to think that the two of you could adopt?"

Conall snorted. "She wouldn't even consider the option. She wanted a baby of her own and she was determined to get one no matter what she had to do."

Vanessa's brows peaked with questions. "So what options did that leave?"

Fixing his gaze to a spot on the floor, he said, "She wanted to go to a fertility clinic and get impregnated by a donor."

"Oh."

"Yeah. I understand that's a suitable solution for some childless couples. But at the time, the whole idea revolted me. I was young and full of masculine pride. I didn't want to see my wife pregnant with another man's child, much less have her giving birth to one. I tried to explain that it would leave me feeling as though I was on the outside of things. I argued that adoption would be a better option for the two of us. An adopted child wouldn't be more hers than mine—it would be ours."

"She couldn't understand your feelings? Or she didn't want to try?"

Dropping his hand from her hair, he released a long, heavy breath. "Nancy was a headstrong woman determined to have her way. She accused me of being selfish and robbing her of the right to be a mother. A 'real' mother in her terms."

Sickened by what she was hearing, Vanessa laid her hand on Conall's forearm. "So she didn't believe an adopted child would be a 'real' child," Vanessa mused out loud. "Well, I could tell her, or anyone, that the twins are just as much my children as if I'd given birth to them."

As he turned his gaze back on her, a wan smile tilted his lips. "Yes. But you're not Nancy. It took me a few horrendous days without you to figure that out." He turned his gaze to the picture window framing the wall in front of his desk and this time when he spoke his voice was reflective and full of doubts. "I suppose I was equally responsible for the breakdown of our marriage. Perhaps I was selfish for not letting her have her way. Anyway, I've stopped trying to figure it out. We wanted different things and nothing could change the way each of us felt."

Her fingers slid back and forth over the warm skin of his forearm as she searched for the right thing to say. "You both had different values and ideas about things. That never works—unless one of you sacrifices everything. And that wouldn't have made you happy, would it?"

"No." His expression pained, he said, "You know, I believed I'd married a woman that loved me, but after a while I realized I didn't really know her at all. And that made me the biggest fool who ever walked down the aisle."

A self-deprecating frown turned down the corners of Vanessa's lips. "Forget it, Conall, I hold that honor," she told him, then asked, "What finally happened? You two could never come to terms about having children, so you agreed to divorce?"

"I wish it had simply ended that way."

"What do you mean?"

"Like I mentioned before, something twisted in Nancy—I don't know what. I'm not even sure a psychiatrist could tell you. But she became an obsessed woman. She wanted to become pregnant. Anyhow, anyway that she could. She kept hounding me about going to a clinic and selecting a donor. I kept refusing and she continued to hound."

"I'm surprised she didn't ask for a divorce," Vanessa mused. "But love binds and I'm sure she didn't want to lose you."

His grunt was a cynical sound. "Nancy probably did love me in the beginning. At least, I want to think so. But after she learned I was sterile, I think all that died. She hung around because she liked being in the Donovan family. She liked the luxuries and privileges, the social standing that went along with the name."

"I see," Vanessa murmured thoughtfully, "Was she originally from a poor family?"

Conall shook his head. "No. Her family wasn't rich by any means, but they were financially comfortable. Nancy was the youngest of three children and I think after the other two grew up and left the nest, her parents doted on her. I'm guessing she learned at an early age that she could bat her eyelashes and quiver her lips and get most anything she wanted. After a while I grew weary of her demands, but I didn't ask her for a divorce. I wanted our marriage to make it and I suggested that we needed counseling to help us work out our problems."

"So did she agree? Did you two go for counseling?"

Rising to his feet, he crossed the room and rested his shoulder against the window frame. As he stared out at the busy ranch yard, he spoke in a flat voice. "She laughed and said that all we needed was a baby to make us happy again. At that time I didn't know what was going on in that head of hers. And I would have never known if Liam hadn't come to me and told me."

Frowning, Vanessa asked, "Liam? What did he have to do with any of this?"

Turning his head, he looked straight at Vanessa. "Nancy went to him and begged him to get her pregnant. In her twisted mind, she was sure that I would accept the baby. After all, it would be a true Donovan, she reasoned."

Vanessa gasped. "That's—insane! And how did she plan to explain her pregnancy?"

His lips took on a wry slant. "Divine intervention. She believed she could convince me that the medical tests were wrong and by some miracle I had gotten her with child. And if she couldn't convince me, then she was gambling that I could never turn away from my own brother's baby."

"How terribly sad," Vanessa said pensively.

After a moment, she went to him and rested her palms against his chest. "Oh, God, Conall, I didn't know that any of this had ever happened to you. Maura or anyone in your family never spoke to me about your marriage or why it ended. And I've not asked. You must have been so crushed when Liam revealed what Nancy had done. And I can't imagine what it must have done to him to have to tell you that your wife...well, that she was disturbed."

He cupped her face with his hands and she was relieved when the dullness in his eyes flickered to a bright and shining light of love.

"Actually, in some strange way the whole incident brought him and me closer. But that was the only good thing to come out of the mess. After the divorce, everything else about me was pretty much numb and I guess I stayed that way until I met you." He lowered his head until their foreheads met and his lips were hovering close to hers. "For years, I got damn good at hiding my feelings. I didn't want anyone guessing that I might be vulnerable or hurting. I didn't want anyone thinking I was anything less than a man. I guess I must have perfected my acting ability. Otherwise, you would have seen how much I love you."

"Oh, Conall, yesterday evening I got to

bring Dad home for a visit and while he was there we had a long talk about you and me. He made me see how stubborn I was being and how much the twins and I were going to lose if I didn't get you back in our lives."

Smiling now, Conall rubbed his nose against hers. "Thank God for fathers. Not more than an hour ago, mine pretty much said the same thing to me."

Rising on her toes, she brought her lips up to his. "And thank God you're going to be the twins' daddy. And if they're not enough to turn your hair gray we can always adopt a whole house full of babies to go with them."

Wrapping his arms around the back of her waist, he clamped her tightly against him. "Hmm. You'd do that for me?"

"Only if you think you can handle the double duty."

He chuckled as he pressed his cheek against hers. "Double duty? I think you'd better explain, my darling."

She sighed as the warmth of his body and the goodness of his love filled her with pure, sweet contentment.

"That you'll always love me just as much as you love our children."

His lips moved to the side of her neck where

he began to mark a trail of kisses. "You're going to quickly learn, my lovely, that I always honor my family duties."

A month later, early autumn had moved in to predict the winter to come. The night air was sharp and clear and sometime before dawn frost would lace the fading roses in Kate's garden. But inside the Donovan ranch house no one cared about the chilly weather. The lights were blazing, music filled the great room and there was no end to the dancing and plates of good food. Family and friends had gathered to celebrate the marriage of the eldest heir of a horse-racing empire and no expense had been spared for the party.

Two weeks ago, Conall and Vanessa had decided they couldn't wait for a big, traditional wedding to be planned. Instead they'd flown to Las Vegas and married in a little wedding chapel not far from the spot where they had first kissed. Afterward, Vanessa had insisted they spend their week's worth of honeymoon, not in Jamaica, where Conall had initially planned to take his new wife, but at Del Mar, where they'd played in the sand and surf and watched Red Garland race to victory in the Debutante. The fact that Vanessa had remembered how

Red Garland held a soft spot in Conall's heart, much less that she'd be willing to accommodate their honeymoon to catch the filly's race, had amazed him. And he knew those special days they'd spent loving each other on the California coast would be relived in his mind on each and every wedding anniversary.

Now, as Conall moved Vanessa around the dance floor to a romantic waltz, she gazed up at him, her face glowing. "When your mother said she was planning a little get-together for us, I was expecting a gathering of twenty to thirty people. This reception is incredible. I never expected to see so many people. So much food. So much…everything!"

Happy that she was so pleased, Conall squeezed her hand. There was never a time that Vanessa didn't look beautiful to him, even in the mornings when her face was puffy from sleep and her skin bare of makeup. But tonight, dressed in an ice-blue concoction that provocatively draped her curves, she looked especially lovely. And as they danced, he kept asking himself why he'd been so blessed, while at the same time thanking God that he had been.

"And I never expected to be enjoying it all so much," he confessed. "Normally when my parents throw parties, I'd always find an excuse to make a quick exit. But not tonight. We're going to dance until dawn."

The sparkling light in her brown eyes warmed him with loving promises. "Just dance?" she teased.

Grinning, he whirled her out of another couple's path. "Ask me that question later—when we're climbing the stairs to our bedroom."

Since their marriage, he and Vanessa and the babies had taken up residence in an upstairs suite of rooms that were connected to his original bedroom. As for the little Valdez house where Vanessa had been living, Alonzo had been able to move back home, thanks to live-in assistance that Conall was only too happy to provide. His father-in-law's health was continuing to steadily improve and tonight the older man was clearly enjoying being here at the party, chatting with friends and acquaintances and watching his daughter dance with her new husband.

As the music finally paused, she said, "I'm having a lovely time, Conall, but would you mind if we took a few minutes to slip upstairs and check on the twins? A couple of hours have passed since Hannah had them down to meet the guests."

"You've been reading my mind," he agreed.

"Let's go give Hannah a little break, so that she can come and enjoy the festivities."

With his hand still wrapped around hers, he led her out of the crowded great room and down a long hallway until they reached a polished staircase. Side by side, they climbed the steps until they reached the second floor. At the end of the landing, Conall tapped lightly on a carved door. When they entered the room, Hannah was sitting at the end of a long couch. The dim glow of a table lamp illuminated the book in her hands.

She looked up in surprise. "Don't tell me the party is already over."

"It's just now getting fired up," he assured the devoted nanny. "We thought we'd better come see how you and the twins have been getting along."

"In other words, you wanted to come up and play with your son and daughter," Hannah teased.

Vanessa laughed. "How did you ever guess?"

Laying her book aside, Hannah gestured toward a nearby door that led into a room that had been transformed into a beautiful nursery. "The last time I peeked in they were both asleep."

His hand still latched around his wife's,

Conall began to urge her toward the nursery. "Get out of here, Hannah. Go on down and enjoy the party. We'll take care of things up here for a while."

The woman glanced down at her jeans and fitted sweater. "I'm not dressed for a party. But I will go down to the kitchen and test the food," she told him. "Whenever you need for me to come back up just let me know."

As Hannah slipped out the door, they both thanked her before making their way into the quiet nursery.

Near the head of the crib, an angel-shaped nightlight illuminated the slumbering babies and Conall's throat tightened with emotions as he leaned over the rail and touched a finger to each sweet face.

"I never dreamed I would have one child," he murmured. "Now I have two."

Vanessa's arm slipped around his back and as always, whenever she touched him, he felt strong and sure of himself. But most of all he felt loved. Utterly loved.

"When we first went to the orphanage to see the babies, you told me then that you were certain you'd never have children. I thought it was because you didn't want any," she admitted. "And I couldn't fit that notion with the Conall I knew and loved."

Rick's tiny fist was lying outside the blanket. Conall picked it up between his thumb and forefinger while imagining how his son's hand would look in a few years after he'd grown to be a man. Other than being a husband to Vanessa, being a father was the richest gift he'd ever been given and he was cherishing every moment with his new family. "I'd already decided that I would never find a woman I could love again, much less one with children. I'm so happy you proved me wrong, my darling."

After placing a kiss on each baby's cheek, he pulled Vanessa over to a wide window that faced the southwest part of the ranch. Through the boughs of the pine trees, a ridge of mountains could be seen reaching up to the star filled sky.

Vanessa sighed with pleasure as he pulled her into his arms and kissed the crown of her head. "See that break in the mountain? Way over to the west?" he asked.

Vanessa's gaze followed his instructions. "Yes, I see it."

"I want to drive you over there tomorrow," he said. "I want you to take a look at the view and see if you like the spot enough to build our new home there."

Leaning her head back, she stared wondrously up at him. "New home? You don't like living with your family here in the big house?"

"I love living with my family. It's the only home I've ever known. But the Donovan family is changing and growing. Brady and Lass already have a daughter and I suspect they're already planning for another baby. And who knows, Liam might shock us all and marry again. Plus, there's Bridget and Dallas. This old house can't hold us all. Besides," he added, as his hands moved to the small of her back to gather her closer, "our children deserve a home of their own, one that they can pass on to their children."

"Mmm. Family tradition. I wouldn't expect anything else from you, my dear husband." She slipped her arms around his waist. "I only ask that our new home be simple and homey. And that you make a big fenced yard for our children to play in."

Smiling, he brought his lips down to hers. "You're such a demanding woman."

She kissed him softly, then easing slightly back, whispered, "How long do you think it will be before our guests realize we're missing?"

With a wicked chuckle, his arms tightened around her. "Long enough."

At the same time, down in the kitchen, Brady was doing his best to persuade Hannah to join the rest of the merrymakers while Bridget was at the far end of the cabinet, holding one hand over her ear while straining to hear the voice on the other end of the telephone.

With her hand over the receiver she scolded, "Brady! Shhh! I can't hear a thing." Turning her attention back to the caller, she finally managed to pick up the sound of a male voice and as she did her face grew pale, and her heart kicked to a rapid thump. "On the res, you said?... Oh....Yes....Yes, I remember....I'll be there as soon as I can make the drive."

When she hung up the telephone, she started toward a door that exited to the outside of the house. Thankfully, she'd left her coat and medical bag in her car and wouldn't have to waste time fetching it or dealing with prolonged goodbyes.

"Sis! Are you leaving?" Brady called after her. Her hand on the doorknob, she paused to glance over her shoulder. "Yes. An emergency has come up."

Leaving Hannah, he trotted over to his sister. "Is it that important? This is your brother's wedding reception," he pointed out, as though she needed reminding.

Tossing him an impatient look, she said, "You know as well as I do that emergencies don't pick and choose their times to happen. Explain to the family why I had to go and give my love to Conall and Vanessa."

"Sure." He gave her a quick kiss on the cheek. "Are you headed to the hospital?"

Shaking her head, she stepped through the door and out into the cold night. "No. But I might end up there," she called back to him.

Before he could ask more, Bridget hurried away from the house. She didn't want her brother to know that it had been his old friend Johnny Chino that she'd been speaking with on the phone. And she especially didn't want Brady to know that she was driving straight to the Mescalero Apache Reservation. He wouldn't understand why Johnny had summoned *her*. And frankly, Bridget didn't, either.

* * * * *

REQUEST YOUR FREE BOOKS!

2 FREE NOVELS PLUS 2 FREE GIFTS!

H HARLEQUIN®

SPECIAL EDITION

Life, Love & Family